# CONSPIRACY

---

BY

JACK FRERKER

To Doug + Nancy - Enjoy!
Fr. Jack Frerker

PAX PUBLICATIONS – OLYMPIA, WASHINGTON

Published by PAX Publications, 7710 56th Avenue NE, Olympia WA



Printed in the U S A, by Bang Printing of Brainerd MN



---

**LIBRARY OF CONGRESS CATALOGING-IN-PUBLICATION DATA**

**Frerker, Jack, 1937 –**

**CONSPIRACY**

**ISBN 0-9740080-3-6: 978-0-9740080-3-5**

---

**OTHER NOVELS BY JACK FRERKER**

**HEAT**

**SOLSTICE**

**CONNECTIONS**

# ACKNOWLEDGMENTS

Thanks once more to the, by now, usual suspects: Garn Turner for a fourth wonderful cover; to Richard Swanson, my electronics guru; and to Paula Buckner and Tom Vickery, as well as new-comer Joe Weir, for their proofing and editing prowess.

I'm also grateful to the team of Green, Lynch and Stone (David, Frank and Steve, that is), for keeping me honest on all the legal points in my story. Saluki grads all, they practice honest-to-goodness law in various locations around Southern Illinois. If you need some legal wizardry, I can hook you up with any or all of them.

I should have long ago thanked my family – over-due as it is – my gratitude to them as well. Their kind encouragement and under-whelmed demeanor is heartening and humbling all at once.

And to you, my readers, whose loyalty may well outweigh your literary good sense, I am once again in your debt. Writing is largely my creative outlet. Your continued support has kept me at it longer and more diligently than I know I would have all by myself.

Jack Frerker

TO JOANNE SWANSON
IN LOVING MEMORY

# CHAPTER I

There was a strange smell coming from Belden Woods.

Jimmy knew it. All his third-grade friends did too. But none of them would speak of it. And none of them would go into those woods any more, even though it had been a favorite haunt. They had excuses ready, should the subject come up. They were grateful that it didn't.

It wasn't fear, of course. Who wanted to see a mess of old, rotten pumpkins or decomposing stumps or whatever else it might be, like a dead polecat? Or worse.

The smell lingered most of that summer, despite several good rains. Puzzling, actually, when you think about it. But each of the boys avoided that. It had occurred to most of them to tell some adult. But they didn't. Definitely out of the question! As was actually going into those trees!

Jimmy almost brought it up to Ricky. Yet he did find reasons to walk past that isolated clump of trees well off the road to the river where they fished and swam sometimes when no adults were around to say it was dangerous. They had been right, the adults had. Gene Melder drowned there a few years later. Having friends with him hadn't helped, either, despite adult insistence on the buddy system as the last resort should they insist on swimming there. Only after Gene's death did the pool that the kids had long wanted finally come to be. Until then, they had to go twenty miles to swim where people weren't so stingy.

Jimmy would occasionally pretend to scour the weeds near the woods for something. By summer's end you couldn't smell anything from the road. Only closer to the trees, he thought, was there an occasional whiff of something. Maybe that's why adults didn't notice: none of them ever got that close. When school started, he forgot about it, and by the next summer, even when he would get off the road and approach the trees, the smell was gone. But he still avoided going in among the trees. Besides, he was older, and there were other things to do and other places to do them in.

By the end of grade school, the memory had faded totally, and it remained out of mind throughout the rest of what he liked to remember as his childhood. College came and went. So did marriage for him and most of his childhood friends. Belden Woods didn't come up again.

Not, that is, until his twenty-fifth year, when a human skeleton was unearthed by a boy's dog. Ironically, the kid was a third-grader, and he was scared silly by the incident. Only then did Jim and his friends remember. And only then did they decide to talk about it for the first time, ever.

# CHAPTER II

They decided on coffee at the truck stop just outside Algoma. Later, they would think it an unwise choice. But at the time, it seemed the thing to do: go where all the town guys went – the *older* guys – to solve the world's problems in a solidly male environment every Saturday without fail, even at holiday times.

They stood out, newcomers and decades younger than the habitués, though they had come early enough that only a few of those men were there before them. The seven pulled together two tables in a back corner. The discovery in the woods had brought them there, but that wasn't what they talked about at first.

Willy, the tall, gangly jokester of the group, wondered why they never gathered as adults even once in a while. They had been thick as thieves in grade school and even high school. When college took them separate ways, they shared e-mail and phone calls and an occasional drink on school breaks. All of them returned to Algoma to marry and settle down, and they attended each other's weddings. But marriage, it seemed, had taken them in separate directions. Still, it was odd, Jim remarked, that they were brought back together by something like this.

That led to happy stories from the early days. But several cups of coffee later Rick called them back to what they had agreed upon in the first place.

"Jim, you called us. What do you know about this?"

"Not much, except that I was aware of an awful odor in that stand of trees the summer after third grade. When I called around, some of you said you'd noticed it too. I thought we should talk. The town's in a tizzy! Whatever the heck happened there, we now know that it certainly wasn't good."

They agreed. Each of them had shied away from those trees and from even discussing the place. Pete allowed as how it was little-boy bravado that kept him from telling anyone. "You think the smell had anything to do with the skeleton?" he asked.

"Probably, don't you think?" Rick said. "Anyway, it can't hurt to tell the police now, can it? I mean, any of you still embarrassed about how we acted as kids? Are you, Paul?"

"No. But what do we know that can possibly be helpful? We smelled something bad once when we were little? Good grief, that was … sixteen years ago!"

"At least it gives them a time reference," Jim offered.

That sounded logical.

"Any of you remember if someone went missing that summer?" Willy had raised a good point.

No one did, and Tom was sure they would have remembered something like that.

Harry, who liked to read mysteries, wondered about the skeleton's sex.

No one had heard.

"They just discovered the thing the other day and haven't had time to check that out, I guess. At least, I haven't heard anything yet," Willy ventured.

"You think it was a mob hit or something? Maybe the body's from out of state! Anyway, whoever dumped it there's long gone,"

Pete said. "Maybe we shouldn't get involved, just in case whoever put it there might not take kindly to our meddling." He had always been skittish.

"Good Lord, Pete," Jim said. "We're just going to say we smelled something sixteen years ago!"

"Yeah, well, don't say I didn't warn you. And don't put *my* name on this," Pete replied.

"And if there's a reward? Still want your name left out of it?" Harry kidded. Everyone laughed but Pete.

That's where they left it. Jim would tell the sheriff. And he suggested that they not be surprised if the law wanted corroboration from them.

After they broke up, Jim stopped at the jail. The sheriff didn't seem to make much of it and never got back to any of them. However, the information did put the investigation on a new tack, given the time suggested by the tip. But even that turned up nothing locally.

The incident became old news before the month ran out, an interesting blip on the radar and nothing more. Soon people were paying as little attention to it as Jim and his friends had to the restaurant crowd that Saturday. In time, the young men would wish they had been more observant.

# CHAPTER III

Algoma had always been sleepy of a summer. The announcement of the skeleton that May shook things up enough that the coming summer might just prove to be exciting. The rumor mill went into high gear and the Smile had headlines for two weeks. But with no further developments and interest waning, the end of the school term seemed destined to issue in another quiet vacation season.

At the body shop that bore his name, Tim Burdin – his ads and business cards bore the slogan *Bodies by Burdin* – was complaining about the dearth of wrecks and fender benders, and he began urging his help to take early vacations. The town swimming pool was scheduled to open after Memorial Day, but the weather wasn't warm enough to coax hordes of children there. And while crops had gotten in on time, the cooler weather was making a good harvest iffy. The only good news was that no gully washers had forced a second round of plantings.

Father John Wintermann still loyally stopped periodically at the Becker pharmacy. He had sworn off ice cream for Lent and hadn't started in again, proud to have lost several pounds that he now wanted to keep off. So he sipped a Diet Coke each time he stepped inside the pharmacy's quiet, soothing interior but usually didn't stay long, given the paucity of news to share.

Fred and Frieda were always pleasant, but they too regarded things as duller than usual. The three had, of course, talked about the skeleton. It was a delightful puzzle at first and even later as it was easing out of prominence, but the incident was shrinking to the kind of oddity not worth long remembrance or discussion.

Two weeks after the discovery, however, a Friday night spree of vandalism involved three cars parked in the same block on Ash Street. It was prom weekend, and the incidents were chalked up to underclassmen excluded from the dance. It occurred in front of three neighboring houses: tires were slashed on the passenger side of two cars. A third car had its front passenger-side tire done in, and a knife was found by the tire, suggesting that the vandal may have been disturbed in flagrante delicto. No one reported seeing the incident, and the sheriff was quoted as saying only that the knife was large and expensive. He also said he was convinced that it was indeed the weapon, since its serrated pattern matched all the slash marks. No fingerprints or any other identifying markings were found on it, and the knife looked fairly new. A check of county stores came up dry, and reports from St. Louis weren't yet available, he reported. While Father John thought those clues intriguing, no one else seemed to, including the sheriff. He hadn't said so, at any rate.

Rick and Harry were two of the victims. The third was an over-the-road trucker who could be found in Algoma when he wasn't taking a load somewhere. All three were upset, but the trucker was particularly vociferous, having little good to say about town teenagers and saying it at the top of his voice to anyone who would listen.

To Rick and Harry, his reaction was of a pattern. Though not a native, the man had lived in Algoma well over a decade, having come from somewhere up north on the heels of an unsettling divorce, it was said. In any case, he lived alone and had little to do with his neighbors or anyone else in town. Little was known about him, consequently, but people had nonetheless seen the darker side of his personality. Neighborhood dogs in his yard and hot-rods on his street had occasioned anger that neighbors regarded as over the top. Toilet paper in his trees one fall provoked a particularly angry response, despite the fact that every home for two blocks along Ash Street had suffered the same fate on a football Friday night. Word went out, and he wasn't bothered again – until the tire incident.

Neither of the two boyhood friends made anything special of the vandalism, however, until Jim Eisner's car suffered a blowout on a bad stretch of highway outside town a week later. He was returning home from work with the federal government in St. Louis. A flextime arrangement allowed some workers to avoid heavy traffic times by going to work early and returning before rush hour. Others, like Jim, went in around mid-morning and came home after the highway congestion.

He usually returned to Algoma around 8, and while it wasn't dark yet at that time of year, it was overcast and rainy that particular evening. His accident occurred on a curve by the creek bottoms and careened his car into the wooded area beside the road. Jim had lain unconscious some minutes before he was able to use his cell phone. No one had seen the wreck or his car in the woods some ten feet below the highway. He suffered a concussion and broken bones but was told that he would recover and that he should consider himself very lucky.

The insurance adjuster declared the car totaled and Tim Burdin sent it to Horace Denver's junkyard. Something about the blown tire suggested to the police that it might not have been an accident, but only the fact of the blowout and Jim's injuries were released to the Smile. Father John learned the rest of the information several days later when he bumped into the sheriff outside the jail.

Standing in the bright late-morning sun of a gorgeous day, one that seemed to promise the warm weather usual to the cusp of spring and summer, he greeted the sheriff. "Morning. You've been busy lately, what with the tire vandalism and Jim Eisner's wreck."

"Sure have, Father. Hope you haven't had to be as busy."

"I haven't, thanks. Anymore, I don't know about our teens. Maybe they don't have enough to keep them properly occupied."

"You mean the Ash Street tires, Father?"

"Sure."

"That may not have been the work of youngsters."

"You don't say! What makes you think so?"

"Several things, actually. Got a minute?"

The priest nodded.

"'Member how well we did puttin' our heads together over Annie Verden last summer? How about helpin' me with this stuff?"

"Sure. I got time."

"Come on in out of this sun. We can sit a spell more comfortably and more privately, too."

After Father John had refused anything to drink, the sheriff picked up the conversation. "It wasn't kids for several reasons. For one thing, the knife was much too weird and expensive. For another, the incident apparently happened way too late at night."

"How do you know that?"

"A neighbor across the street got in after 2 and only saw two cars parked out there. When he closed his bedroom blinds before going to bed around 2:20, he still saw only two cars. And the prom curfew was a little after midnight, so it's not likely there was any kids wandering around two, three hours later. I haven't quizzed all the parents, but I'd stake my career on that, especially when you add in that blade."

"The knife was that strange?"

"The short answer is yes. Wanna see it?"

Father John soon realized what the sheriff meant. The knife was bone-handled, long and thickly bladed, and it had an ominous-looking serrated edge. "This sort of thing expensive? Looks it to me."

"Yes, and not much good for the ordinary user. I'm told it would be good on large ocean-going fish or animals like elk and bear. Myself, I can't imagine it being any good around here. So it strikes me as not the kind of thing a high school kid would believably have in his possession."

"I'm inclined to agree. But then, how explain the vandalism?"

"I can't. Not easily. Certainly not before Jimmy's accident."

"Oh? They were connected, you think?"

"Not that I can see for sure yet. But what I mean is that something else about that wreck has raised my suspicion."

A deputy popped his head into the office about a call on line two.

"S'cuse me, Father."

"Want me to step out?"

"Maybe not. Let's see what it is."

The call was routine, and sheriff Lawrence Toler motioned for Father John to stay. "Thanks, Phil," he said. "I'll get back to you."

He turned back to the priest to explain. "More on Jimmy's car, but nothin' important: no fingerprints, 'ceptin' Jimmy's. Where was I? Oh, yes, the tire. Its tread was intact. It wasn't anythin' he ran over."

"So how'd it blow?"

"Something punctured the side of the tire, Father. It's very unlikely the tire was defective, because the whole set was only months old."

"How could that happen, then? Unless something was pushed into it! But not at fifty miles an hour … "

"It could if something were shot into the tire."

"Was there a bullet?"

"No bullet. Not in the tire or elsewhere. We put a metal detector all over the area from the skid marks to the crash site. No bullet!"

"I'm lost," the priest said.

"So was I 'til I noticed something on the tire lining opposite the puncture area. We recovered most of the tire, you see. What we found was a rather small and peculiarly shaped indentation."

"So?"

"Didn't know what to make of it at first. Then I thought of the small hole in the skull of the skeleton from Belden Woods – that too was puzzling when I first saw it. But I got to thinking that something like whatever caused the hole in the skeleton's head could have punctured that tire. I mean if it was a lightweight projectile, it might not make it through both sides of the tire. And the splattery indentation on the tire wall might just fit that assumption."

"What're you saying, Sheriff?"

"That if I'm right, whoever killed that unfortunate person might still be at large … and around here, at that!"

# CHAPTER IV

"That's weird," the priest said, shuddering.

"Yes, and I want to brainstorm with you precisely because it is."

"Okay, but first let me ask. How did you get from the knife to the hole in the tire?"

"Jim Eisner came to me about the skeleton. He told me that he and his gang of grade-school buddies all knew about a strange smell in Belden Woods some years ago, and they figure now that it had to do with that skeleton."

"Did it?"

"Probably. Almost certainly."

"And the tires?"

"Rick and Harry were two of the gang of buddies."

"Am I jumping to conclusions, or do you think these two otherwise-separate incidents were retaliatory?"

"It has occurred to me."

"But the third car doesn't belong to any of that bunch, does it?"

"No. Plus, the man's not from Algoma originally and he's older than they are."

"So … ?"

"So I'm asking you to help me brainstorm."

"Okay … "

"So, what do you think?"

"Don't know, offhand. You got anything for starters, Sheriff?"

"I figure the user of the knife has to come from elsewhere."

"Why would someone from out of town want to slash tires?"

"As a wake-up call to the guys who talked to me, of course. They *did* identify the time the skeleton guy probably died. Someone, I figure, might not have liked that, and perhaps that someone's from out of town – or connected with someone out of town."

"But why slash a tire on that third car? And how did an outsider find out about what Jim and his friends had given you?"

"The third car may mean the vandal wasn't sure who owned which cars. If he was an outsider, that's believable. Or it may be a deliberate red herring. Maybe the vandal knew exactly who owned what, and the third car's an excellent way to throw us off while he still gets his message to the intended targets. Right now, however, I'm not sure how someone from out of town – if that supposition's correct – found out about the guys. But remember: the skeleton did make the news, and not just here in town."

"None of that gives me a eureka moment," the priest said. "And what about an outsider finding out about Jim? His name wasn't in the paper."

"Maybe the slasher and whoever knew about Jim aren't the same person! What if someone in town knew about Jim and got an outsider to slash the tires – to throw us off?" The sheriff looked expectantly at the priest.

"It would protect his identify. But if that's the case, then you can't rule out any of Jim's friends, including Rick and Harry. They all knew Jim came to you."

"Yes, but that's not likely. They were kids at the time the skeleton guy died, and what motive would they have? Nothing like that makes any sense, however remotely possible it might be."

"Nor to me, either, frankly. But you have to keep the possibility in mind."

"Okay, but it's not high on my list," sheriff Toler said.

"Where's that leave us? Seems like a lot of information and an impossibly large a list of suspects," the priest said.

"Not necessarily. I'm tracking down that knife, as we speak."

"Are you planning to talk to all of Jim's friends?"

"No, why?"

"To warn them, if nothing else. Anyway, who knows what you might turn up talking to the lot of them? I'm planning to see Jim in the hospital, by the way. I wanted to give him a day or two to recover his wits, so to speak. Mind if I gather his friends informally after talking to Jim?"

"Not at all, but the hole in the skeleton's skull and the stuff about Jim's tire are off-limits."

"Okay. But let's us talk about the skull a moment," Father John said. "What do you think it could be?"

"Not sure. It's not a big hole and matches no bullet profiles I'm aware of. And, like at the accident scene, we found no bullet in the skull or nearby. Can't rule out the possibility that the person was killed somewhere else, though, and then brought here. Also, the hole wasn't that deep in the skull, so I don't know what a pathologist might say about its role in the person's death. A projectile that size could have blown Jim's tire, and it's interesting that it didn't make it out the other side of the tire."

"Male or female skeleton, Sheriff?"

"Its size makes me think male. Don't know enough anatomy to judge otherwise. Should know soon for sure, though."

"Well, if whatever made the hole didn't kill the person, what did?"

"Beats me! I'm hoping it was the cause of death. I can always do a search for smaller bullets. But with only a skeleton to go by, we may not be able to determine the cause of death. And not finding a bullet, I'm in a quandary. Will you think about that too, Father?"

"What about missing persons? Too long ago to check that out?"

"No, but it won't be easy. No one from around here fits the bill, and checking elsewhere may take a real long time. But we've started doing that now. About all we may have to go on are dental records. No DNA records from back then, sorry to say."

The priest nodded and rose. "I'll let you know if and when I puzzle out anything. Meantime, we know how to reach each other." Waving goodbye, he left for St. Luke's in Burger.

# CHAPTER V

Father John greeted the information desk attendant and inquired about Jim's room number. Then he asked about other patients from St. Helena's.

"No one besides Mr. Eisner, Father."

"Hadn't heard of any either, Gladys. Have a nice day, and say hello to your mom," the priest said, as he turned toward room 122.

Father John rounded the corner and almost bumped into Doctor Wilson. "How's Jim Eisner, Doctor? I'm on my way to his room. A little heads-up would be nice before I see him."

"And how are you today, Father?"

"Fine, thanks."

"You coming to see me sometime soon? It's been a while."

"I could. Guess I've forgotten to make annual visits a priority. But you'll be glad to know that I lost some weight this Lent. And so far I've kept it off. Five pounds or so."

"Good! Looking forward to seeing you. As for Jim, I was a little worried about his concussion, but he seems to be coming along. Told him he was lucky."

"So, nothing to really worry about?"

"I'd say that now, yes. Why?"

"Just wanting to know how to approach him. Don't want to say or do anything uncalled for."

"Give him some good cheer, Father. He'll be happy to see you."

"Any advice about how long to stay?"

"Not unless you're planning to be there more than an hour."

"No, nothing like that. Just want to say hello."

"Go get him, Father," the physician said and wandered down the corridor toward the ER.

Father John knocked gently on Jim's door and entered.

"Come in, Father," Jim intoned surprisingly strongly. "I was hoping you'd come."

"Really?" Father John winked at the smiling patient propped up in bed. "Don't want confession, do you? Maybe anointing? When I first heard, I had visions of using the oils on you. But the hospital never called – which was happy news, I guess."

"Takes more than this to bring me to the edge," Jim said, grinning again.

"Don't tempt fate, young man," Father John replied. "Life can be pretty fragile at times, you know."

"No need for the lecture. I've already had it from my wife. *And* I've learned my lesson, in case she brings it up to you."

"Actually, now that I see how well you seem to be doing, perhaps I could switch gears. What do you remember about your accident? Anything?"

"Pretty much everything, except for the time I was out."

"And that was how long?"

"How would I know?" He grinned. "Best I can figure is maybe ten minutes, give or take, before I used my cell phone."

"And … ?"

"And what?"

"And what do you make of it all? Bad luck, or what?"

"Bad luck, yes. Why do you ask?"

"I heard the tires were new."

"They were. And, by the way, I got word from Horace Denver that I should salvage the other three before he formally accepts the car and pays the insurance company a pittance for it. But is that important?"

"I just thought new tires wouldn't be such easy prey to road debris," the priest said, hoping he wasn't being too obvious.

"Don't think it matters much. If you run over a big enough piece of something, I think any tire'd buy the farm."

"That what happened? Ran over some metal?"

"Guess so. Haven't really been told and haven't thought to ask. I was more interested in my own health, frankly. Though I did have Peg ask about the insurance stuff."

"What'd she find out?"

"The car's a total loss. We need another one. And the money won't pay for a new one. But then, this car was used when I got it before our marriage, and I've had it four years now. In a way, it's good to be rid of it, although I can think of easier ways." He grinned again.

"It's just that I heard the tire's tread is intact."

"What do you mean?"

"The tire tread wasn't damaged."

"No holes in the tread?" Jim sounded totally incredulous.

"So I heard. Horace Denver would know, I imagine. Maybe Peg could check on that for you." Father John was keeping a poker face firmly plastered in place.

"So could I – we! Why don't you call him right now, Father?"

"If he'll answer. You know he's not always there, Jim. And I'm not sure how reliably he answers his phone, when he is."

"Please – do me the favor," Jim said, pointing to the bedside phone.

"I'll need the number. Got a phone book here?"

A quick search proved fruitless, so Father John dialed the front desk. Moments later he reached the junkyard and was surprised to hear Horace's voice.

"Father Wintermann, Horace. Got a moment?"

"Sure, Father. What can I help you with?"

"I hope you've been okay. Haven't seen you in a long while. I understand you've got Jim Eisner's car."

"Sure do. It's right messed up."

"I'm sure it is, dropping off the road into the creek bottoms like that. I guess he's lucky he's not as messed up as the car. What I was wondering is, can you tell me about the tire that blew? I heard the tread's okay. That correct?"

"Yep."

"Then how could there have been a blowout?"

"It blew sideways, Father. Bad tire, I guess."

"Strange! The tires were new, weren't they?"

"The other three are. That one too, judging from the tread. Think I also heard that from someone. Maybe his wife. She called about the car. Anyway, the tread isn't worn much at all."

"Sounds strange, but I guess even new tires can be lemons. You have a nice day, Horace. And, by the way, next time you're near the rectory, ring the bell. I'd like to chat about Annie's artwork."

"'Kay, Father. Bye."

Father Wintermann hung up and looked at Jim. "Were you able to figure out what he was saying, or you want me to go over it?"

"Go over it, even though I think I got it."

"He said the puncture didn't come through the tread but from the side of the tire. The tires *were* all new, right?"

"Yeah. Only two, three months old."

"Horace thought so. Think you got a defective one?"

"Guess so. Why you dwelling on this?"

"Heard you told the sheriff about the skeleton. Did I hear right?"

"I'm guessing you heard that from the sheriff, and if so, then you know you heard right. What's this all about?"

"Rick Binz and Harry Grant had their tires slashed. They're part of your 'skeleton group' too, aren't they?"

"They are. But what are you getting at? That someone's got it in for us all?"

"I'm just putting two and two together, Jim. I don't think it's a stretch to consider that *may* be the case."

Jim sat stunned. "Hadn't crossed my mind."

"Good thing I brought it up, then. Could be wrong, of course, and a few more weeks might demonstrate that, if nothing else occurs. But just in case it is true, it couldn't hurt to have a little confab with your friends, could it? Maybe one of them's got an idea who could be ticked off about your talking to the sheriff. Better safe than sorry, no?"

"Yeah! What do you suggest?"

"Why not talk with everyone? And sooner rather than later – maybe even here in the hospital."

"Good idea. With any luck, they can get here tonight. Can you come too? You seem to have a mind for this sort of thing, coming up with something that didn't occur to any of us, like that."

"If you insist."

"I do!"

"Then I will. Tell you what, if they can come around 7, I'll show up at 7:30. You'll have time to talk without me, and when I get here, maybe all you'll need me for is to critique things. Okay?"

It was agreed and, after giving Jim his blessing, Father John left for home.

# CHAPTER VI

On the way back to Algoma, Father John decided to brief sheriff Toler. Accordingly, on his return to town, he pulled up in front of the courthouse and crossed the street to the jail. The sheriff was expected soon, so he made idle conversation with the desk sergeant and learned that two cars had recently hit deer in the southern part of the county. Both men agreed that was odd, such things usually happening in the fall. Father John wondered whether out-of-season hunting might be stirring up the deer population. The deputy allowed as how that was possible but didn't seem much concerned.

When the sheriff appeared, it took Father John less than two minutes to relate his hospital room conversation. "I didn't say anything about the tire lining. Let's see what the group comes up with tonight."

"Sounds good. Stay in touch."

"You too," the priest said and made his way to his car. Having already decided on his next destination, he pointed his aging Ford toward Tim Burdin's shop on Front Street.

"How's business, Tim?"

"Not so good, Father."

"I guess you didn't have much to do on Jim Eisner's car."

"Nothin', really. Just sent it on to Horace, once the insurance company agreed to total it."

"I was wondering if you had a chance to examine it."

"Yeah. Why?"

"Anything wrong other than the blowout?"

"You mean, steering or brakes – like that?"

"Yeah. Anything to cause a crash and blow the tire in the process?"

"Nothing else indicated, Father. Anyway, weren't there skid marks?"

"I think so, yes, but that would be true in other scenarios, like locked brakes or hitting a deer, wouldn't it? I just found out that there've been a couple of deer incidents in the county of late."

"In some cases, possibly. Anyway, no brake or other problems."

"Just wondering. Talked to Jim and, while he says he remembers everything before going unconscious, I thought he could have been shook up and, you know, got it wrong. Might have been something other than a blowout – 'cause the tires were so new. So he says, and Horace too. Makes me wonder about it being a blowout."

"Oh, blowouts are weird. Even new tires can be defective in ways not obvious 'til they go out on you – and Jim's were definitely on the new side. No, it was a blowout, all right. The tread indicated he didn't run over nothin'. The tire blew out the side."

"Well thanks, Tim. Glad to get it from the horse's mouth. You'll be glad to know Jim's doing okay. Forgot to ask just when he gets out of Luke's, but I'm guessing soon. 'Course, that broken right arm will trouble him some – keep him from work for a while – not to mention the broken ribs. See you in church, Tim." He smiled and turned to leave, knowing Tim would catch the irony. The odds weren't great the two would see each other the coming weekend.

Father John vetoed stopping at the Becker pharmacy and made straight for home. There were no messages, so he caught up on the St. Louis paper and had some chicken noodle soup and a ham sandwich. By the time he left for Burger he was fed, rested and up on the latest.

He was surprised at the number of young men in Jim's room. He had convinced himself there would be only three, maybe four. Six were crowded around Jim's bed, all talking at once. Rick Binz noticed him in the doorway and shouted hello. Everyone stopped talking to look.

"Didn't mean to bust up the party," the priest said, smiling. They laughed and made room as he moved toward the bed to shake Jim's good hand. "Come up with anything?" he asked no one in particular.

"Not much," Willy volunteered. "But I was wondering if anyone found out whether the skeleton was a man's or a woman's?"

Father John was about to say that he didn't know, when Paul Leubel said it was definitely male. Father John wondered why the sheriff hadn't seemed as sure. Maybe Paul was just passing on the latest rumor.

"So, what do you make of that?" he quizzed the group.

"Don't rightly know," Rick said, after everyone had looked at each other. "Anybody hear of a guy going missing when we were in third grade?"

No one had.

"Anybody know how he died?" Paul asked.

The silence indicated another blind alley.

"Wonder when they'll put that out?" Tom Bigger asked. Generally the quiet one, for him to speak at all was something of an event.

"Gotta be soon, don't you think?" Rick said. "Anybody got an in with the police? Maybe you, Paul? You heard about the skeleton's sex. Where'd you get that from?"

"A deputy who lives on my block. He was fetching his garbage can when I got into my car. But we're not all that close."

Father John decided to explain his presence, in case Jim hadn't already. "I was here earlier today, and Jim and I were wondering if someone was out to get you all for talking to the sheriff."

"Yeah, Jim mentioned that," Willy said.

"Well, what do you think? I told Jim I'd come back tonight in case you had some ideas."

"Only thing we can figure is that someone heard us at the truck stop, Father," Rick said. "The sheriff's the only other person who could finger us, and it couldn't be him."

Father John looked around the room at the nodding heads. "Who was at the truck stop, then? Anybody remember someone who didn't fit or looked suspicious?"

"We were talking about that just now, Father," Willy Peters said. "No one we noticed seemed suspicious but, then, we weren't especially looking for that, either."

"Any strangers, people you didn't know, people from out of town?" Father John asked.

"Of course, Father. Truckers stop there all the time. But I couldn't say how many were there that day," Harry said. Harry Grant was a plump-faced young man, the recently married one of the group.

"Well, then, who was there that you know?" Father John pursued.

Again it was Harry. "The usual older guys, although, as I remember, only a few. I guess we were somewhat early for the whole crowd – fifteen or twenty guys, I think." The others were nodding in corroboration.

"Like who?" Father John prompted.

"I only remember one table: Joe Schmitz, Hank Daley, Bill Grimmer and Harold Bittner, I believe," Harry said.

"And Gale Smith came in a little later, right?" Rick Hahn said.

Several others agreed.

"And you don't suspect any of them?" Father John said.

"No," Rick said. "But I guess we can't totally rule them out."

Jim spoke up, and Father John realized that he had been silent thus far. "Been thinking about that before everyone got here, and I can place only several more there: Smitty, the counterman, and Jerry, the cook, of course – and Jack Eppner. But he was settling his bill when we came in. He left before we got seated, so it couldn't have been him."

"Anyone else, Jim?" the priest asked.

"No. And I've racked my brain about it."

"And the rest of you?" Father John asked.

The silence was not encouraging.

"I'm trying to remember the guys at the counter," Paul finally said. "All I come up with is that they were truckers. They were friendly enough, chattering away, as truckers do, I suppose, in places like that. Any of you pay attention to 'em?" he asked the group.

A chorus of denials greeted his question.

But then Rick asked: "Harry, am I mistaken or was Gib at the counter?" Gilbert Wetzel was their neighbor and a trucker. His car had the single tire slashed when Rick's and Harry's cars were vandalized.

"Now you mention it, I believe so," Harry said.

"So what? He got a message too, if that's really what the tire thing was all about." Pete Hamilton had waited to put in his two cents. The resident cynic, he could usually be relied on to dampen a conversation.

"That's not the point," Rick said. "Maybe he can identify other locals or even some of the truckers."

"You got a point," Pete conceded. "Gonna check with him?"

"I can," Rick said.

"So can I," Harry added. "One of us will get to him for sure."

"Good," Father John said. "Am I right, then, we have nothing besides Rick's and Harry's neighbor?"

Jim said, "I haven't heard anything else. Right guys?"

The group around the bed nodded in assent.

"Then I'll be going. You all keep cheering up the patient," Father John said to the group, "and let me know if you come up with anything new. I sure hope we're wrong about our fears." He gave his blessing to all of them and left.

On his return to Algoma, however, try as he might, Father John could not escape the sinking feeling that their paranoia was appropriate.

# CHAPTER VII

Hearing nothing for several days, Father John thought of calling Rick or Harry. He would see Jim again, if nothing developed soon, but before he could do that, Jim called him to say that he had been released from the hospital. With the doctor no longer worried about his concussion, he would complete his recovery at home, he said, and added that he had heard nothing from his friends in the interim.

Communion calls that Thursday and Friday plus homily preparation and weekend Masses to boot preoccupied Father John, so it wasn't until the following Monday that he could turn his attention back to the young men.

He was grateful for the nice weather. It could be very warm already in May, but this year it had turned out quite pleasant. A very comfortable spring thus far had been making for open windows, especially at night. It was also the kind of weather that allowed for walking around town, which was what he was doing Monday morning when he saw Horace Denver in an alley several blocks from the rectory. He waved for him to wait there until he could catch up to him.

"Glad I saw you, Horace. Been wanting to ask about Miss Annie's paintings. Any luck selling them?"

"Yep. In Philadelphia."

"Was that where you'd sold them for Miss Annie too?"

"Same place. Has me send three or four every month or so, and ever so often I get money when he sells any."

"You trust him, Horace?"

"Why not? He always sent money before."

"You believe he's being fair, Horace? He's awfully far away."

"I do, Father."

Father John had always found reading Horace's face difficult. Today was no different. Apparently the junkman trusted the art dealer. He hoped Horace wasn't being taken advantage of. *Perhaps Annie worked out the original negotiations, and all Horace had to do was continue doing business with the same man. Has to be it!*

But he also wondered how much the paintings were going for and what Horace was doing with the money. Knowing Annie, she had probably spelled that out, too, in the letter Horace received when the estate was settled. *It's really none of your business, John. Let it go!*

As an afterthought, he inquired how Horace sent the paintings to the dealer.

"By truck."

"Suppose so. What I meant was, are they packaged specially?"

"They told me 'zactly how to put 'em in a wood box, Father."

"That would be a crate, right, Horace?"

"Think so."

"How long's it take them to get there?"

"Don't know for sure. Few days, I guess."

"Sounds right. Well, thanks, Horace. No need to stop at the rectory. You've answered my curiosity. Thanks again."

Small talk with Horace was never easy.

The priest continued on uptown. He had the weekend collection to deposit and wanted to see Fred and Frieda for any recent news. It might even be time to try a little ice cream. Then, remembering the doctor, he vetoed that idea. But he would stop at the pharmacy, anyway, after the bank, just to stay atop the gossip.

He waved to Maisie Brown inside the bank and said he would see her soon when she came to clean the rectory. He was nothing but happy with her work, and she seemed pleased to be working for him. He quickly made his deposit and was about to make his way out, when Bob Lanner's secretary, Bobbie Sue Langley, came out of her office, motioned for him to wait and made her way to where he was standing several feet from a teller's cage.

"Mr. Lanner says to tell you hello, but I wanted to chat a moment myself. I think it's just awful what happened to young Jim Eisner. The buzz is that it wasn't an accident."

Father John barely contained his surprise over how that had leaked out. For Bobbie Sue's sake, he raised his eyebrows. "You don't say. Where'd you hear that? When I saw Jim in the hospital, he didn't mention that." He was glad that he could be literally truthful.

"Mr. Lanner mentioned it to me. Don't know where he heard it. But if it's true, what ever could be going on?"

"Most anything, I guess. But as nice a young fellow as Jim is, it's strange he should have enemies."

"What if it's connected to that skeleton in the woods?"

"You think it might be?" Father John mustered as disingenuous a look as he could.

“Mr. Lanner thought so. Anyway, since you’ll probably see Jim before I do, be sure to tell him he’s in my prayers. And if you don’t want to alarm him, perhaps you shouldn’t pass on what I just told you.”

“I’ll be circumspect, Bobbie Sue. But I’m curious where Mr. Lanner heard that. It’s certainly disturbing. Give Mr. Lanner my greetings, please.”

He blew her a kiss as he made for the front door of the bank, already resolved to test that news with Fred and Frieda without tipping his hand. He also determined to call Bob Lanner as soon as he could. Someone in the sheriff’s employ is sloppy if not untrustworthy.

The Beckers didn’t volunteer anything about Jim’s accident, so the rumor wasn’t very widespread yet, Father John figured, and he redoubled his intention to call Mr. Lanner as soon as he could. There wasn’t much other news, except that the Gilliams won some money in the ship’s casino on their recent cruise. He told Fred and Frieda with a wink that he hoped they would be tithing on that to the Methodist Church.

As soon as he got back to St. Helena’s, he called the bank and was put through quickly to its president.

“Hello, Mr. Lanner. I hope you’re feeling fine. Talked to Bobbie Sue a few minutes ago. Perhaps she told you. I was wondering where you heard that Jim Eisner’s wreck might not have been an accident.”

“Doing well these days, Father. Thanks for askin’. Heard that from one of the deputies who was here inquirin’ about a home loan.”

"If you don't mind, I'd like to verify that with sheriff Toler. We've been on pretty good terms ever since Annie Verden's death. I'm sure he'll be frank with me. My own feeling is that, first of all, that's very disturbing. But secondly, I'd bet anything that the sheriff wouldn't want something like that bandied about. Let me check with him. Meanwhile, why don't you and Bobbie Sue just keep that to yourselves 'til I can get back to you."

"Okay by me, Father. I'll wait to hear from you."

"Thanks. You can depend on my calling you back soon."

Within moments, he was talking to the sheriff and relaying his recent discovery, along with his suspicion that the word hadn't gotten around the town yet. He asked the lawman what should be done.

"We sure don't want that on the street, Father. I'll call Bob Lanner myself, tell him we just spoke and make sure he knows to keep that to himself. I'll also reassure him that it's important enough that we are pursuing *all* the possible implications of that new 'rumor.' Then I'll find out which deputy let it slip. We'll tighten up our ship here, all right. Glad *you* heard it and not someone else. No need for you to call the bank, then. I'll do that. *And* our arrangement still stands: contact each other the moment either of us uncovers something. Correct?"

"Right, Sheriff."

"Thanks for getting to me. I'll stay in touch."

After he put the phone down, Father John wondered if Bob Lanner or Bobbie Sue had told anyone else. He hoped not. He also hoped that the sheriff would make sure about that.

*What a sticky mess this is turning out to be!*

# CHAPTER VIII

Spring in Algoma and throughout all of Southern Illinois can bring summery temperatures. So far this year, it had been everything from quite cool to, more recently, thoroughly pleasant. But it wasn't yet what you would call hot. The nicer weather ensured that windows in Algoma would often be open. Willy Peters' certainly were later that same evening.

A little past dark, just after 9, Willy and his wife were standing in the center of their living room discussing their grocery list when it slipped from his hand. As he stooped to retrieve it, there was a small crash on the wall behind them, and the glass on the French Impressionist print hanging there shattered.

Too startled to think clearly, it took several seconds for them to piece together what had happened. Something had come through the open window, zoomed past where his head had been just seconds earlier and broke the glass covering the print. Finding a small hole in the screen, they looked outside but saw nothing suspicious. They then went to the print and stepped carefully around the glass on the floor beneath it. The print was largely intact except for a small but deep hole in the matting near the print's edge. It appeared that they would be able to remount the picture.

Only then did they call the police.

Two deputies were soon taking their statements and examining the scene. Minutes later sheriff Toler joined them in their living room. Both police vehicles had arrived without sirens or flashing lights, so the five were able to talk without arousing the neighborhood. The sheriff didn't mention Willy's membership in the "skeleton group" but soon asked if either Willy or Betty minded Father John joining them.

As the priest arrived, the deputies were reporting that the line of fire between window and wall suggested that the shooter had been crouching outside more or less at the height of the window ledge. But the lawmen were puzzled to find no bullet or bullet casing. The sheriff and priest exchanged nervous glances when they heard that from the deputies, who also reported summoning the forensics team to check for fingerprints, footprints and the like.

As the others continued to talk, Father John moved over to the wall hanging, taking care not to disturb the scattered glass. He noticed a small wet spot inches from the wall, and quickly deciding to share that information only with the sheriff, he took out his handkerchief and bent down. Appearing to scrutinize the array of glass, he quickly blotted the damp spot and then pretended to wipe his forehead as he stood up. He sniffed the cloth on its way back down from forehead to suit pocket and then rejoined the others as the couple was finishing a summary of everything they had given the deputies.

The group was soon able to bid Willy and Betty goodnight, the sheriff promising to share any information they might get. But Father John and the sheriff noticed Willy's face. It was clear that he now believed someone was targeting him and his friends.

"Feel free to call, Willy. Even tonight, if you'd like," Father John said as he stepped outside.

"Just might, Father."

"Give me thirty minutes to be sure I've gotten home."

"'Kay," the young man said, feigning a calmness that he didn't feel. Outside in the young night, the sheriff ordered his men to wait for the forensics team; then he and Father John walked in silence to his police cruiser. They talked only after the car door slammed shut.

"You spotted something?"

"There was a bit of clear liquid on the floor beneath the picture. Sopped it up with my handkerchief." He sniffed it again before handing it to the sheriff. "My guess is water. Looked like that inside, as well."

The lawman sniffed and agreed. "What do you make of that?"

"Beats the heck out of me! But with no bullet here, not even a BB, and none in Jim's tire or the skeleton – what about ice? It's the only thing I can figure. Makes no sense, but it's something to consider. Can you shoot ice?"

"Don't know, but I'm sure as hell gonna find out! Give me a day or two. Right now, though, you best get home. I'll give 10-to-1 Willy's gonna call."

"Sure 'nuff. But am I right: this water-ice thing's off-limits too?"

"Yep."

"Want my handkerchief, just in case?"

"Can't hurt."

Father John was soon beside the rectory phone. It took Willy another fifteen minutes. It was a long conversation.

# CHAPTER IX

The next morning, Harry called from work. He had gotten hold of Gilbert Wetzel. While they talked one evening recently, Gilbert had helped fix Harry's timing belt. But he hadn't proved much help. All the guys at the counter that day had been truckers, and he knew none of them.

It seemed another dead end.

But Father John pressed Harry. "What's he prefer to be called: Gil, Gib, Bert, Gilbert? And was it a long conversation? Must have been, if he helped fix your car. What all'd you talk about?"

"He doesn't like Bert, but everything else seems to work. We talked about this and that – a lot of small talk. But I did find out that he really knows engines. He should, being a trucker and all, I figure. He must have had his share of breakdowns in the middle of nowhere."

"Doesn't fix cars for other guys on a regular basis, does he?"

"Don't think so, but he could, I suspect. He was pointing out all kinds of things under my hood."

"Did he run at the mouth about the tire slashing?"

"No, and I'm glad he didn't get all riled up. But he did mention that he's been pretty busy with his truck runs."

"Yeah," the priest said, "but he was in town the day you talked to him."

"And the day before too, I think, because I saw his truck where he always parks it."

"You heard about Willy's house last night, I guess."

"No, what?"

"Somebody shot something through the front-room window while he and Ann were talking. It missed them but broke the glass on a picture hanging on the back wall," Father John said noncommittally.

"You don't say!" Harry said, adding after a slight pause: "Got something to do with the skeleton, maybe?"

"Willy thinks so. He called me later and we talked a pretty long time." Father John omitted the fact that he had been at Willy's place with the sheriff.

"This is getting scary! Pete – you know: Pete Hamilton – was concerned about just this sort of thing at the truck stop. Maybe he was right."

"A few precautions might be good. You may want to make sure everything's locked up good and tight."

"That's for sure. Think I'll call Willy too. Do the other guys know yet?"

"I don't know. Wouldn't hurt to give them all a jingle. But it strikes me that while you all should take care, it's not clear exactly what to be worried about. Heck of a situation!"

"Right. On both counts! I'll call 'em all, plus the sheriff, I think."

"If you want," Father John said, "but Willy's probably the best guy to talk to sheriff Toler, since they're no doubt staying in touch about the vandalism."

"Yeah. Okay. I'll sort it out with the guys, then. Good talking, Father. Bye."

Father John had no sooner hung up than the phone rang. It was Jim Eisner.

"Hello, Father. You seen this week's Smile?"

"Can't say as I have. Doesn't come 'til tomorrow."

"Well, I got little else to do – this recovery's so darned slow – so I take walks around town. I was uptown this morning and stopped at the Smile to get a copy hot-off-the-press, so to speak. Front page has something about my wreck maybe not being an accident."

Masking his distress, Father John asked with no little surprise: "What's it say?"

"Little else than that. Seems there's a 'rumor' goin' 'round. Doesn't say how or where it started, but the short article indicates that the Smile is trying to determine its accuracy."

"You talk with Herb?" the priest asked.

"No. I just picked up my copy and continued my walk. Didn't really look at it 'til I got home just now."

"Wasn't Herb around? You'd think he would have talked to you, if not before he printed that thing at least while you were there!"

"Didn't see him. But ain't that just like that damned paper – pardon my French, Father – to print something like that without talking to the people involved!"

"Well, frankly, yes it is, Jim, sorry to say. But don't go getting all steamed up. That won't help your recuperation. Let's approach this calmly."

Father John believed that somehow the bank conversation had leaked out, and he was trying to think about the next logical steps for him and the sheriff, as well as for Jim and his family – the whole skeleton group too, come to think of it. He continued to converse with Jim. “Was there *nothing* about the origin of that ‘rumor’?”

“Not a thing, Father.”

“You talk to the sheriff about this yet?”

“No. You’re the first one I called.”

“Why not let me do that, then? There’s other stuff you might want to attend to, like Willy Peters. Hear about his home last night?”

“What?” Jim asked, alarmed.

“Something came through his front window. No one was hurt, but a picture was damaged. Could have been kids. Willy’s shook up. And I heard from Harry just moments ago, too. His conversation with Mr. Wetzel didn’t turn up anything. When I told him about Willy, he thought you all should talk. May want to get hold of him, although he just might be trying to get you right now. Sorry to shake you up some more, but best you all deal with this stuff rather than put your collective heads in the sand!”

“Thanks. I’ll call him. Will you let us know what the sheriff says?”

“You can count on it. But stay as calm as you can, Jim.”

Father John put the phone down and hovered over it a few moments before picking it up again. “Sheriff Toler, please.”

The sheriff’s voice soon came on: “Can I help you?”

“Father Wintermann, Sheriff. Just heard from one of the young men. They saw Gilbert Wetzel in the restaurant that morning, and one of Gil’s neighbors – Harry Grant – has asked him if he knew anyone at the counter. He didn’t. They were all truckers passing through. Another blind alley, but I thought you’d wanna know.”

"Appreciate it."

"Doesn't help much, I guess, but you never know! I was also wondering about the deputy who spoke to Mr. Lanner at the bank. Ever learn who that was?"

"Name's Hank Winstrom. Been my deputy almost a dozen years now. Came from Chicagoland and had already been to the FBI Academy. I suppose you know they train law enforcement people from all over the country at their facility in the D. C. suburbs. Anyway, he's got experience and good credentials – even ran against me my first election. I kept him on the force after he lost. No hard feelings on my part, and didn't seem to be any on his, either. I wanted his expertise. By now he's my right-hand man."

"Am I right or what: talking to Mr. Lanner like that was a strange thing for such an experienced man like him to do?"

"On the face of it, yes. I asked him about that. He said it just slipped out."

"It may have slipped a little too far. Jim Eisner called just now to say that he got the latest Smile on his walk uptown today. The front page says there's a 'rumor' his wreck wasn't an accident."

"What!" the sheriff shouted.

Father John jumped. It was almost as if the man had leaped through the phone. "That's right. And Herb – you could almost predict it, you know – didn't even talk to Jim beforehand. He doesn't seem to have talked to you, either. Unless he got that from your deputy ... "

"I am hopping mad … "

"Well, before you do anything else, lower your voice. No need to spread this to others in your office. Let's talk about that deputy a moment. You know, there are lots of possibilities here. First off, it just defies common sense his blurting that out like that. Secondly, maybe, just maybe, Herb got it elsewhere. Someone may have heard it at the bank and then told Herb. Maybe you should talk to Herb first."

"Yeah. Think you're right."

"And maybe you need to scrutinize that deputy some more. Something just doesn't smell right."

"We'll see. I'll call Herb. I don't care how fast and loose they play with facts at the Smile, this has gone too far! Hank'll be after that."

"You'd also better figure out what to say when people start asking about it. Maybe something could be put into the Smile as well, though you'll need to be ready sooner'n their next edition."

"Right again. Any quick ideas?"

"You can't lie, but you might skirt things a bit. What about: 'We're looking into all possibilities, and whoever suggests that we've *definitely* questioned the accidental status of Jim's wreck is all wet'?"

"Well, we're not *certain* with regard to Jim's wreck, all right … "

"That's what I was thinking … "

"And that *might* shut people up … "

"Let's hope! By the way, I told Jim I'd call you. Want me to say anything to his group about this?"

"Yeah. I'll get something like what you said to Herb, and that's what I'll be saying if anyone asks. But tell those boys to keep their mouths shut. Far as they know, we got nothing more than the wreck happened and seems to be an accident. They shouldn't go stirring up things by acting scared or especially by speculatin' publicly on their own."

"Will do, Sheriff. Keep me in the loop, please."

"I will. Later!" the sheriff said and hung up.

Father John sat by the phone for a few minutes before calling Jim. The line was busy.

# CHAPTER X

Henry Lohman is his Christian name, but everyone calls him Hy, not Henry or Hank. He owns and operates a small grocery store and despite not one, but two, much bigger supermarkets in Algoma, he has managed to stay in business because of the superior quality of the meat he offers. Actually, it's not just the meat but especially his meat cutting skills that brings him customers. Unlike the precut stuff packaged by wholesalers and offered at most stores, Hy's meat is cut to specification from full sides of beef and pork. He was one of a nearly lost breed of butchers still giving the personal touch that was available everywhere not that long ago.

He sells groceries and sundries as well, but it's the meat that has given him his competitive edge, and he has vowed to stay in business as long as he can. In his late sixties, his excellent health suggests that will be a long while yet, especially since none of his children have any interest in keeping the store after their father steps down. So, even though the store's days are ultimately numbered, it enjoys a brisk trade.

It was to Hy's old brick-front store that Father John was headed the next morning, in search of a nice roast and perhaps a juicy slice of ham. Large handwritten signs on butcher paper proclaiming the latest sale items were plastered around the periphery of the two plateglass windows, on the front door and even on the brick-work front of the ancient building. Father John was happy to see one about rump roast. He pushed the door open and took a deep breath to enjoy the wonderful aromas swirling everywhere inside this marvelous commercial space.

Hy's voice was thundering: "Take care of Mrs. Geller, please."

That was for Jimmy, Hy's middle-aged clerk and general gofer, who was, no doubt, tending to shelves in aisle three or four because Father John could see Mrs. Geller coming down aisle two as he stepped into the otherwise empty first aisle. It was a summons for Jimmy to man the sole checkout counter at the store's front.

A large refrigerated meat counter spanned the width of the building at its rear, and before Father John could reach it, Hy's large frame appeared in full view behind that cooler. He was beaming.

"So nice to see you, Father. What you hankering for today?"

"I was glad to see outside that rump roasts are on sale."

"Indeed they are. But let me ask: What do you want one for?"

"To eat, of course."

"I mean, you entertaining, or do you want something mainly for a nice meal for yourself and then sandwiches for later?"

"Sandwiches. How'd you guess?" He smiled as he finally reached the front of the cooler.

"Well, then, I suggest a top round. They're not a sale item, but I'll make you a price," he said, smiling.

"Show me a few, Hy." While the butcher brought forth three roasts, Father John said: "I think I might also want a nice ham slice."

"Can do, Father. Here are several nice ones. I think you'll like the middle one best. It's not too big and looks like it should be nice and tender."

"You've made a sale, Hy. And the ham slice … something less than a pound?"

"You got it, Father."

While the butcher prepared the two packages, Father John perused the other contents of the large cooler but selected nothing more. "Been busy today?"

"Not overly. Kinda quiet, actually."

"No news, then, I guess," the priest said.

"Well, I did hear that Jim Eisner's wreck wasn't an accident."

"You did?" The priest stifled a groan. "Who said so? The Smile?"

"One of the deputies – Winstrom … Hank Winstrom – was here getting some hamburger."

"He just up and said that?"

"Nope. But I told him I saw it in the Smile, and he agreed it was so."

"Definitely? Or just a rumor, like the Smile said?"

"Not sure. He just agreed with me."

"Wonder what that means," Father John said.

"Don't know. But it sounds kinda strange. Can't think of anybody who has it in for young Eisner."

"Me neither," Father John said. "You take care, Hy. Sorry I can't stay to chat. I'm off on parish business. It's a shame, since I'm not often here when you've got time to talk."

He made his way to the front as Jimmy was finishing with Mrs. Geller, paid his bill and was gone in no time.

*This is getting serious!*

# CHAPTER XI

Right after putting the meat away, he called the jail. "Have you talked with that deputy since our last conversation, Sheriff?"

"No. Why?"

"Hy Lohman tells me he stopped in for some meat and, when asked about the Smile's 'rumor,' said it was true."

The priest could almost see the lawman's face turning red. Before he could respond, however, Father John added: "I'm beginning to wonder about that man."

"And I'm beginning to agree with you, Father," the sheriff said, with barely controlled civility.

"Tell you what: You think on it, and I'll be over in a few minutes. This needs some talking over, I'm inclined to think."

"Better still, I'll come to your rectory. Give me a few minutes."

"Front door'll be open. Just come on in."

Father John went to his favorite living room chair, plopped down and began to review things. No new insights or clarity had emerged, however, before the sheriff's voice sounded in the front lobby.

"Where are you, Father?" the sheriff shouted.

"Living room, Sheriff."

He rounded the corner. "Ain't this the damnedest, Father?"

"All the more reason to think it through. Sit down and get comfortable. Who knows how long this'll take. Want anything to drink?"

"Nothing, thanks. Don't have all the time in the world, but I'll take your offer of a chair. That one looks soft." After the lawman settled in opposite the priest, both men sat staring at each other.

Father John broke the silence. "This is getting complicated."

The other man nodded.

"Can't figure your deputy. From all you say, he's way too experienced for that."

"My sentiments, too. May have to consider administrative leave."

"Have you said that to anyone?"

"No … "

"Good," Father John quickly interjected. "Let's think a bit, first. That sounds drastic … like what you do only when there's evidence to check on – evidence, I mean, of something more than rumor mongering."

"Perhaps, but this kind of stuff can compromise investigations, and just on general principle I won't have it goin' on."

"I can see that. But perhaps there are other ways without … *alerting* him. Who knows if he's involved in something about that wreck – or, worse, something bigger! God forbid, and against all presumptions too, but … anyway, maybe there are others ways."

"I *could* put him at a desk. Of course, I'd have to tell him why."

"At first glance, that looks better. What do you say to him?"

"That I can't have that going on, and that I'm slappin' his wrist 'til he learns his lesson."

"I like that, but … "

"But what?"

"Won't he be in the perfect place to see what you're up to? He'll be right in the nerve center, not?"

"Good point."

"So … ?"

The sheriff hesitated. "So I'll just have to be careful, I suppose."

"Can you be?"

"I think I can."

"Well, then … you gonna do that? Put him on desk patrol?"

"Yes! I am," the lawman said decisively.

"So that's settled. But what about the next piece, checking on him? How do you do that? I mean, what's involved?"

"Not exactly sure, but we can start by checking phone and money records – you know, bank account, credit cards, etc."

"And that will tell us … ?"

"If he *is* up to something, it'll almost certainly involve money. It's a place to start. Maybe *the* place."

"Can you just do that?"

"I can with a warrant."

"And can you get one?"

"Well, one way – and it avoids Hank listening in, too – is to get either FBI or state guys involved. But I'll still need that warrant."

"Is that easy – or even possible – to get them involved?"

"We'll see. I'll start by talking to Judge Monroe."

"Hugh Monroe?"

"You remember – last September … Annie!"

"Sure, I remember. But he's retired. Can he get you a warrant?"

"No. But he knows the best way to get one," the sheriff said, smiling.

"You're pretty sly, you know."

"Thanks for noticing," the sheriff said, grinning again.

They left it at that, plus a promise to keep Father John informed.

# CHAPTER XII

Just after noon, Father John learned that Deputy Winstrom was now at a desk in the sheriff's office and that Judge Monroe had not only told sheriff Toler how to get his warrant, but also which judge to approach. But the first thing, the judge had said, was to check out the state police. That done, the warrant would be easy.

Things were moving off center. Time would tell if anything would justify the search. But Father John wondered what the sheriff could say to his deputy if nothing turned up. He also wondered where all this would lead if something *did* surface from the investigation.

Before anything could emerge about the deputy, however, there was new activity with the skeleton group. Later that same day, Pete Hamilton's car went off the road, and he was in the Burger hospital.

Father John arrived within minutes of the call to his rectory and anointed Pete in St. Luke's emergency room. He emerged to tell the young man's parents, who had just arrived, that things looked grim.

"He's barely able to breathe, so they put him on a ventilator. There are broken bones and, I'm guessing, internal injuries. I'm obviously no doctor, but don't be lulled into thinking he'll be all right in no time. It's very serious, and I'm sorry to have to tell you that."

Father John hunkered down with the distraught parents for the next half-hour, waiting and praying with them. The doctor finally appeared to confirm Father John's report. They could see their son, he said, but warned that he wasn't responsive and that the prognosis wasn't good. They left Father John immediately for their son, who was now in a room on the second floor.

Shortly afterward, the sheriff arrived.

"We've got a witness to part of what went down with young Hamilton. He saw an older-model red car battering another car from behind on the highway west of town. Turned out to be Pete's, and he was apparently on his way from work in Belleville right around 6. The guy was coming the other way, and before he rounded a curve and lost sight, he saw the car bang Pete's really hard twice. He called 911 on his cell phone, and we sent a cruiser. It appeared deliberate, the man said. A deputy's getting a full statement right now.

"We found Pete's car in a field two miles away. It had rolled over a couple of times, and Pete was thrown clear. We got him over here right away and put out an immediate bulletin for a car fitting that man's vague description. Didn't take long to hear of a car fire several miles up from Pete's accident. No one saw it leave the road or start burning. The firetruck came in time to keep it from total destruction, but you can't tell its color. The front end, however, was punched to pieces. It's got to be the right car! Funny, though, no driver anywhere!"

"What are you saying, Sheriff?" Father John asked.

"Looks like somebody tried to kill Pete and then destroy the evidence. I'm also guessing it's a stolen car. We're processing the plates and VIN now."

"This is way beyond just bothering those young men. We've got a murderous dude running around, Father."

"Think we need to talk to the others?"

“Definitely. It’s gettin’ near bedtime, I suspect, but we need to do it right away. Can you get ’em to your rectory … now?”

“A couple of calls should do it. Will you be there?”

“Of course. That’s what I had in mind.”

After one phone call, Father John turned back to the sheriff, who had been on his own phone. “Ten or fifteen minutes! We should all reach the rectory about the same time.”

“Okay. Let me fill you in on a couple of other things first. Just confirmed it. The car was stolen. A twelve-year-old Pontiac that went missing yesterday a couple of counties east of here. The fire pretty much destroyed everything else useful, however. Way I figure, the driver got picked up at the scene. We may be dealing with a gang.”

“Complicates things even more, right?”

“Yes. And we haven’t got lead one on suspects! But the other irons in my fire … the state just got started on Hank’s finance and phone records. The FBI can’t get in it. No federal law’s been broken.”

“So you’re doing nothing on Hank from your office?”

“Right. But he sure was miffed when I told him he’d be riding a desk for a while, so he’s probably suspicious.”

“But without anything going on in your office … ”

“ ... he shouldn’t be able to find out anything. And if he *does* tumble to something, the state guys won’t cough up diddly to him.”

“Good. Think they’ll find anything?”

“Hard to tell. In a way, I hope not. I want to get to the bottom of this, but I sure hope he’s not involved.”

"I can understand why you'd like to keep him ... "

"Exactly. You go on ahead to Algoma, Father. I'll be there in a few minutes. Tell them about Pete. I'll tell them everything else."

# CHAPTER XIII

Father John had just gotten inside his rectory when he heard the front-door bell. It was the first two of the young men, and before he could even begin to tell them about Pete, the bell sounded again. When they had all finally assembled moments later, he gave them the sad news.

"Can we see him?" one wanted to know.

"That's up to the doctor – it might be possible. But Pete's not responsive and his condition's quite serious. His folks are with him now. But before you even consider heading to Burger, I have to tell you that sheriff Toler wants to talk to you all. He's on his way here, and I'm guessing we won't have long to wait."

He walked out of the room to allow the young men to fret among themselves and admitted the sheriff into the kitchen through the rectory's rear door a few minutes later.

"They're in the living room, anxious as all get out."

"Nothin' new. Let's go talk to them," the lawman said.

The sheriff wasted no time. "I have troubling news. Pete was apparently deliberately run off the road. We know *the car* that did it, but not *who.* The car was stolen, and we found it on fire several miles east of Pete's accident."

"Are you sure it's the one?" asked Willy.

"We got a 911 call from a fella heading the opposite direction. He said an older-model red car was bashing another car really hard from behind. Said it happened twice before he lost sight of it. He wasn't able to help with a description of the driver but thought he saw only one person – no passengers. The burnt car has a real-banged-up front end, and its plates and VIN confirm it's a stolen vehicle. Pete's in serious condition. I don't know his prognosis." He looked at Father John. "You hear anything more on that?"

The priest shook his head no, but added: "It's not good."

"Well, then," the sheriff said, "I don't know about trying to see him, which I guess you'd all like to do. Best talk to the doctor, or you might make a trip for nothing'. Although, his folks are there, and you might want to see them. Anyway, concerned as I am about Pete's condition, I'm here because I'm just as concerned about all of you.

"Since we haven't found the driver of that car, my considered opinion is that we got us one serious problem here. Someone not only tried to kill Pete, but used a stolen car and then torched it to destroy whatever might help us. I figure an accomplice picked up that driver – which means there's a gang after you all, not just an individual. And they're not just tryin' to aggravate you. They're willin' to kill."

Turning to Jim Eisner, he said: "Given all this, I now believe your wreck was no accident, Jim. Put it all together: your wreck, the shot through Willy's window, this here incident. We've got a killer loose in the county, and I'm sorry to tell you we have no idea who it might be."

The men in the living room were in shock.

"What do we do, Sheriff?" Jim asked.

"Take extreme precautions with your vehicles. You also need to make sure your homes are locked and secure. But, since we don't know anything about this perpetrator, I admit that I'm at a loss about what else to tell you. It's hard to say if or how they might come at you, or who of you might be next. Report anything out of the ordinary to me. And I'd be thinking about sending your families out of town, if I were you. We'll beef up patrols around your houses, but we can't provide anything like twenty-four-hour-surveillance."

There was a stunned silence. The phone beside Father John's chair shattered it suddenly. Several of the young men jumped.

Father John listened in silence, his face slowly turning sad and flinty at the same time. When he replaced the receiver, he turned to the group. "The hospital says that Pete's been coded twice. They pulled him back once, but the second time doesn't seem to be working. His folks have been told to consider whether to keep him going with all the tubes in him, or … "

There was a wordless gasp from the young men.

"I've been asked for, so I'm leaving right away. My guess is that you may just be in the way, were any of you to come. But who am I to say you can't? Just lock my front door when you leave, please. Sheriff, will you be joining me?"

"I think not, Father. Nothing I can do there. So I may also 'just be in the way,' as you put it."

"Understood. I'm off, then. I can't tell you all how sad I feel for Pete and his family, and for all of you. Feel free to call over the next few days … any time. Whatever transpires at the hospital, I'll get word to you."

He was at St. Luke's fifteen minutes later, sitting with a heavy heart next to the Hamiltons, who hadn't yet made a decision about what the hospital staff was asking of them.

After an agonizing hour and a half, Pete's parents decided that there was no more hope and reluctantly authorized the removal of all the tubes and devices from their son. Father John reassured them that it was all right and accompanied them as they said their goodbyes to their only son. The young man hadn't responded for almost three hours by that time. Nonetheless, after removal from life support, he lasted nearly ten minutes. Priest and parents kept vigil at his bedside and all three were holding his hands when he stopped breathing.

Father John helped them through a very slow and difficult Our Father and then drove the numb couple home, promising to have someone bring their car from the hospital the next morning. He privately doubted that they would get much sleep the rest of that long night.

# CHAPTER XIV

Preparations for Pete's funeral consumed the next two days of Father's John's week. He had no time to check on Pete's friends or the precautions they might be taking. He finally saw them on the night before the funeral at the wake, where the whole town seemed to have turned out to say goodbye to the young man and to console his family.

Before venturing into the room that held the casket, Father John talked with the two Feldspar brothers to get the lay of the land. They had taken over the mortuary when their father stepped down some years earlier and presented a generally less flamboyant profile than their father had. Father John got the general picture from them about who was there that night, names of family members, some of whom had come some distance, and the special arrangements requested by the family. Then he asked: "How's your dad?"

"Fine," the elder brother said. "He'll be driving the hearse tomorrow. He likes that, and it's a way to keep him involved. He loves retirement but never hesitates to drive for our funerals."

"It'll be nice to see Larry again. Seems like the only time we get to talk is in the front seat of that beautiful Cadillac of yours," Father John said and smiled gently. "I'll get with the family now, if it's all right," he said and moved into the large viewing parlor.

He made his way slowly through the crowd, easily greeting cat-lickers and pup-lickers alike. He knew everyone, except for the out-of-towners. He should. He had been pastor at St. Helena's for nearly thirty years, working with Catholics and non-Catholics on various projects and committees in their little town, as well as marrying and burying his cat-lickers, baptizing their children and ministering to them in happy times and sad. This was certainly one of the sadder times.

He hoped no one would raise the issue that he and the sheriff were agonizing over. Burying a young man in the flower of early manhood was difficult enough without worrying the whole town about someone stalking the young man's friends. So far as Algoma knew, Pete was simply the tragic victim of a one-car accident. Thus far, the few who knew otherwise were to keep that to themselves. He hoped the lid would stay on that can of worms at least several more days.

Parents and relatives stood in front of Pete's casket. Father John reached them quickly and spent the better part of the next hour there, occasionally greeting those who filed past to offer condolences to Pete's family. When he was finally able to move away, he went straight to Pete's friends in the rear of the room.

They looked grim, although most people saw that as sadness. The six were talking in hushed tones as he approached, and he kept his own voice quiet as he spoke to them.

"You okay?" he asked, glancing about the room to be sure they were able to talk in privacy.

"No," Jim said in dead earnest. "This is tough."

"I'm sure it is. But what I especially meant was … "

Willy cut in: "That's not good, either, Father. We're all batching as of this morning. Our wives and kids are out of town. We've even discussed whether we should be too. A couple of us could and still not miss work. But that won't work for Rick and Tom, and it doesn't seem right to leave them here at the mercy of God-knows-who or -what." The remainder of the group nodded. "Besides, we're not sure that'll solve anything. If someone's out to get us, he'll still be after us whenever we think it's safe to return. It's a hell of a pile of quicksand!"

Jim jumped in. "Anything from the sheriff? He hasn't called us."

"We haven't talked, either. I've been tied up with this funeral," Father John said, his mood darkening. "You know, I've got wonderful health – no dyspepsia, even. But this last day or so, I wonder if I'm not coming down with an ulcer. This is really getting to me. I can only guess what it's like for you." He continued glancing about.

"You looking for someone, Father?" Tom asked.

"No. Just making sure we're not being overheard, or even especially watched. You think you guys are paranoid," he said with a gentle smile that he thought better of almost immediately. "I hope you've been alert as you've been talking back here."

"Matter of fact, we have," Paul said. "It's an awful way to live, as Willy suggested."

"Well," the priest added, "the sheriff does have a few angles he's pursuing. But, as I said, I haven't heard of any progress since the rectory. I figure I can check in with him tomorrow after the funeral. Meantime, no news is good news, I guess. Nothing's brewing we need worry about, or I'm sure he'd have said something. Keep me posted, won't you? I'll do the same. See you tomorrow at the funeral."

He turned to go, but then turned back. "It should go without saying that you're all in my prayers. But it probably doesn't hurt to make sure you know that. Bye."

They nodded appreciatively as he went to sign Pete's book before the rosary. By 9 he was at home and polishing his funeral homily.

# CHAPTER XV

The morning of the funeral dawned very pleasant. A cool westerly breeze stirred the trees, and an absolutely gorgeous light blue sky stood ready to help them say goodbye to Pete. The all-too-typical hot, sticky weather had yet to set in, and Father John was grateful not to have profuse perspiration distract from the rituals.

Funerals and weddings were special moments for his people, and he wanted to perform them as well as he could. Not fancying himself much of a preacher, he tried to be sure that what he felt for the people came through. He could touch their hearts, if not their minds. That was vastly more important than he believed anyone who might critique his efforts could guess. Truth to tell, he didn't much care what such a person might think. But what his people felt at times like that was of enormous importance to him. Today's effort was no different, and he was happy to see that the weather was more than cooperative. One less thing to distract him.

The funeral went well, despite being such a sad affair. More eyes than the immediate family's were damp throughout Mass, and he knew it had little to do with what he said about the young man. He hadn't tried to eulogize Pete. An uncle performed that service. What Father John spoke about briefly was hope: how difficult but how necessary a virtue it was, and how important for everyone to work on at a time like this. It wasn't inspired, he knew, but it was heartfelt, and he believed that came across to the congregation.

The ride to the cemetery with Larry Feldspar was less jovial that most such trips, but the two men still had a chance to catch up on each other's lives. Larry seemed to sense that Father John was very emotionally invested in this particular death and steered the conversation away from jokes and frivolous topics. Later, Father John wondered just how much Larry knew about what was going on with Pete and his friends. Perhaps nothing, he concluded. But it wasn't their usual kind of drive to the cemetery, and he was grateful for that.

Graveside prayers were brief. As the bulk of the mourners retreated to their cars, Father John stayed on with the family to watch Pete's casket be lowered into the grave. He was surprised at that choice and also surprised that they were able to watch with dry eyes. He returned with them to the parish hall after being assured that they would call whenever they felt the need for comfort or prayer.

The mourners had already begun the funeral meal by the time Father John arrived. Neither he nor the parents were hungry, and they nibbled at their plates of funeral hot dogs, slaw and hot beans.

When he finally got back to the rectory well after noon, he returned a call that his secretary had left for him, changed clothes and only then sat down to contact the sheriff.

*Wouldn't you know: he's out! Wonder if it's anything to do with the skeleton crew.*

The sheriff called two hours later to report nothing new about either Hank or Pete's wreck. The good news, he said, is that nobody was bothering the young men.

# CHAPTER XVI

The next day, the phone at the rectory rang shortly after morning Mass.

"Hello."

"This the priest?"

"This is Father Wintermann, yes."

"Will you be there the next few minutes?"

"Yes, I'll be here. Why?"

"I'll be right over." The caller hung up before Father John could find out what he wanted.

*Now, who was that? Don't recognize the voice.*

Eight minutes later, the rectory doorbell sounded. The man standing outside was a stranger to Father John.

"You the priest?"

"I am. Did you just call a few moments ago?"

"Yes. May I speak with you?"

"Sure. Come in. Such a nice day, pity we're not outside!"

The visitor didn't respond. Both men settled in the small office just off the lobby, and Father John asked how he could help.

"I'd like to make a confession."

"Fine. How long's it been since your last one?"

"Well, that's a little complicated. You see, I was Catholic as a kid, but I haven't been to church in a long while, for reasons you'll understand as I tell my story. And that's the best way to go here, I think, if it's okay, to tell my story."

"Whatever makes you comfortable."

"Well, from the beginning, then. I grew up in Joliet in a Catholic family, as I said. My older brother and me went to school at St. Raymond's Cathedral our entire grade school. My brother went to Catholic high school too. But, since that was expensive, when I got out of eighth grade my folks sent me to public high. That's neither here nor there, really, except that during my brother's high school years he began acting strange. He graduated and everything, but he didn't hold any jobs for very long, and he didn't make many friends, either.

"Near the end of my senior year, he took me out drinking one night. I was underage, but there were lots of places us young guys could get served at and, anyways, my brother was old enough and knew the bartender.

"That night he told me his big secret, about why he wasn't like he used to be. A teacher had molested him when he was a sophomore. And it happened several times before he was brave enough to threaten to tell the principal.

"I didn't know what to think or do. I thought it might be the alcohol talking. And maybe in a way it was, because it probably allowed him to tell me. But there it was, ugly as hell and, like I said, I didn't know what to say. I finally tried to console him, but he wasn't having any of that. He said he was angry, and he also said that ever since then he couldn't get back to feeling the way he had before.

"I eventually got my wits about me and began asking questions. Over a long night of drinking I learned that he never told anyone else, not even our parents, that he didn't know how to get back at the guy, even though he wanted to, and that he was unhappy as hell. I was composed enough to tell him to get help – someone professional. But he turned that down too. Too embarrassed! I asked about Mom and Dad, and he said that I'd better not tell them if I knew what was good for me. I asked why he was tellin' me. His answer surprised me.

"He'd wanted to a few years earlier, to protect me from that sort of thing. But he figured I was maybe too young to hear it. And anyways, I was in public school where that particular teacher wouldn't even know me, so maybe I'd be lucky enough to avoid anything like that. Turned out okay, and he was glad. But he decided to finally tell me because we'd been close before and we weren't any more. He wanted me to know why, and he hoped maybe we could be close again. But then he said he wasn't sure if he wanted to keep living anymore."

The priest's face showed all the anguish he had begun to feel, and when the man paused for breath, Father John spoke up. "I'm so sorry to hear this. It must have been a terrible burden all these years."

"It's not the half of it." He paused, as if summoning up more courage before continuing. "I don't know what I said after that, but I remember talking nonstop for the longest time, my brother just sittin' there listenin'. He even stopped paying attention to his beer. I thought I was getting through to him about quitting those negative thoughts, and when we finally left the bar that night, I was convinced I'd turned him away from some awful brink he was on the edge of.

"But that wasn't the case. Two weeks later he didn't show up for work. When his boss called my folks, they explained that Joey had moved out recently, but they'd check on him. They found him dead in his apartment bedroom, with a gun in his hand. They were beside themselves with grief, and so was I. The funeral was very difficult. And I don't think my folks, especially dad, ever got over it. Even so, I never told them what I had learned from Joey.

"I decided to do what my brother couldn't bring himself to do: get that teacher. But I was smart enough to know I had to plan it really well. So I played with it in the back of my mind for a long time.

"I knew who he was because Joey told me his name. He was still teaching at that school. God only knows if my brother was his only victim. Nothing had ever become public about others, but in my book, one victim was enough. Was too many!

"I made it my business to find out everything I could about him. He had joined the faculty as a young man, never married and wasn't active socially – a tall, slender, nerdy-kind of guy who taught history. He seemed an average teacher, the kind who'd never attract attention, could melt into the woodwork and last forever at most any school.

"I never had a desire to go to college so, after high school, I got me a job with a trucking company out of Chicago. Some of the guys there were gun enthusiasts, and I used to go shooting with them on weekends at a club in the south burbs. One of them introduced me to the company's owner. He belonged to the same gun club and was also a gun collector.

"Eventually he had me and a friend from the company over to his home to see his collection. One of the guns was unique. It shot pellets and used gas to do that." The man didn't notice Father John's eyebrows twitch at the mention of that.

"The gas was in a small container – I don't know what it was called – maybe a 'cartridge.' The owner showed me that it could be attached to a special glass container and, using regular water, you could make seltzer for drinks with it. The gun itself was neat and certainly different, maybe even odd. But it gave me an idea.

"I'd read comics as a kid, and for a while I collected them, especially old editions. I remember a Dick Tracy story in which a villain used a gun like that with an ice bullet to off someone. At first, Tracy and crew couldn't figure out how the guy died. Only when they lifted up a lock of the corpse's hair did they see a hole in the skull. No bullet – just a hole! Well, they eventually figured it out and got the guy. But I was thinking I could do something like that to the teacher, and it could be a perfect crime. I asked to borrow the gun for a few days to shoot rabbits. The owner gave me a funny look but agreed."

Father John's face was beginning to register his growing awareness that he was hearing the confession of a murderer. Even so, he continued to listen in silence as the man continued without pause.

"I took the gun home and experimented making ice pellets the proper size. I couldn't get it right before I had to return the gun, but I was making headway. When I returned the gun, I made the mistake of telling the owner I was trying to make ice pellets work in it. I wanted his permission, I guess. I didn't want to ruin the weapon.

"It was a crude thing, by the way. Looked homemade and probably was. It was several clunky rectangular plastic pieces, though the gun's bore was metal and imbedded in the long piece that formed the barrel. The gas container was in the handle, and you loaded the pellets from the top of the barrel just in front of the firing mechanism.

"Anyway, the owner looked a little surprised when I told him what I was trying to do. He asked me why I wanted to do that. I must have turned red and I know I stammered for some seconds. When he smiled and said it was okay, I didn't know what to think. I hadn't said what I *really* wanted to do, but there he was, suddenly all ears. Then out of nowhere he said: 'Dick Tracy. The ice-bullet killer!' I was stunned that anyone else would know, let alone remember, that story.

"He smiled and said he'd help me perfect the pellets. I didn't know what to say, and I hoped he hadn't seen completely through me. He kept talking about helping with the experiment, and he also spoke of letting me in on some special truck runs that would make me a lot more money. It was very confusing, and before I really knew what was happening, I agreed to meet him the next weekend to work on the pellets. Looking back, I'm sure he had a pretty good idea generally what I was up to. I'm also sure he'd found a sure-fire way to get me to do those special runs for him: blackmail, if it needed to come to that.

"Anyway, to make a long story short, it took several weekends to perfect the pellets, test them and make everything ready. In the meantime, I told him more or less the whole story about my brother. He encouraged me, sayin' people like that shouldn't be allowed to continue that sort of stuff. After we'd gotten the gun to work, he told me about the truck runs that would make me the extra money.

"I was to bring stuff from down south directly to his home, though later there were other drop points too. He didn't say what was being shipped, and I figured I didn't want to know. In time he did say, but it was too late to back out then, 'cause he could talk about me'n the gun. I was drug running for him! But the money was sure good – and still is."

A moment went by. "But I'm gittin' ahead of myself."

"So I tested the gun several times. Then I went looking for that teacher. By then, three years had gone by since my brother's death. But I was finally ready."

He paused for a breath. Father John continued to sit silently, waiting for the story to resume.

"He was easy to find, the teacher was. He hardly ever left his house except for school. He was there the Friday night I went looking for him. After he let me in, I pulled the gun, set him down and explained myself at some length. At first he wouldn't say anything, but I finally got him to admit remembering my brother. When I convinced him how serious I was, he admitted what he'd done to Joey. I never asked if there were others. Joey was enough.

"I made him kneel on the floor and told him to pray. He never begged for his life or anything. Maybe he figured I couldn't actually do it. I gave him a few moments and then shot him in the back of the head. I thought I'd killed him. I'd brought several large trash bags and some towels, and when I began to stuff him into the bags, I realized he was still breathing. I guess I'd given him a concussion or something. But now what was I going to do? I brought only one pellet – keeping them cold was a lotta trouble. I felt stupid and panicky.

"I stuffed him in the bags anyway and dragged him out to my car in the secluded driveway alongside his house. Luckily, he didn't weigh much, so I could hoist him up into the trunk. It wasn't that far a drive to my place, where I put him in the company truck. I still didn't know what to do and wasn't thinking very straight or I might have tried shooting him again – I had more pellets in my freezer. I guess maybe I figured by that time that the gun wasn't powerful enough or something.

"Anyway, that's when I thought to call my boss. He told me to drive to his place right away. When I got there – it took close to an hour – the teacher was still out cold, and we sat down to figure out the next move. He asked if there was any blood back at the guy's house. I told him I'd brought towels and caught what little there was before it could stain anything. And then I used alcohol to clean the area around where he fell. I'd wrapped the towels around the guy's head, and they were still in place when we opened the bag to check on him. I told my boss that I was careful not to leave any kind of mess and that I locked the guy's house when I left.

"Over the next fifteen minutes or so we hatched the rest of it. He gave me a really beautiful set of knives, told me they were mine now and said I should use one of them to slit the guy's throat. Somehow shooting him had been no problem, but slitting his throat was! Maybe it was the blood, I'm not sure. The owner had to talk a while to convince me it had to be that way. Once he explained how to do it all without getting caught – and since I'd come that far anyway – I agreed.

"We dragged him to the bathtub, slumped him over the side with his head inside the tub … and I cut his throat. He bled for the longest time. So long, in fact, that I had to leave the room to let him bleed more or less dry before I could clean him up, and the tub too. My boss helped me, but it was my deal, Father."

The man raised his head – he had been staring at the floor – and looked plaintively at the priest. "There's more, I suppose you've guessed."

The priest nodded, and the man continued.

"He – the owner – said I needed to dump the body somewhere, and we spent some time going over that. We could kill two birds with one stone, he said. I guess I winced when he said 'kill.' He chuckled, I remember. Anyway, he said I could take the first special shipment that night – cash, apparently, though whatever it was, he'd put it into a small box – and deliver it to Mount Vernon. I didn't know where that was, but he showed me on a map. He said that if I hurried – it was near 10 by then – I could get down south before dawn, bury the body and still get to the delivery spot at a reasonable time. I assumed it would be a truck terminal, but turned out to be a house in the town.

"He gave me bags of chemicals he used on his lawn and told me to put some of the stuff under the body in the hole I'd have to dig, and some on top of it. He also gave me a spade and a couple of shovels, and he said that if somehow I couldn't get it done before light, I should make the delivery, get a motel room and bury the guy the next night. Finally he gave me a couple of battery-powered lanterns.

"That was one long drive down to Mount Vernon, let me tell you! I had lots of time to think. I wasn't sorry about killing the guy, but I *was* startin' to worry about gettin' caught. I also realized that I hadn't really thought through what to do with the guy after I killed him. In a way, it was lucky callin' my boss … even though I got hooked into somethin' I was definitely unhappy about, at least at the time. But, you know, after a few years, when I'd apparently gotten by with the killing and was also making all that money, I stopped worrying.

"Anyway, on the drive south that night, I realized I needed someplace well off the interstate. So I got down in this area, turned off and headed west. Between Burger and Algoma, I found a patch of woods near the river, and I was able to finish before dawn. Then I got back on the interstate and kept going to Mount Vernon. The delivery went without a hitch. I was back that Saturday afternoon, delivered a package to the owner and told him how well it went. And that was that!

"From then on, I made a run every few weeks. Besides Mount Vernon, I went to Carbondale, sometimes Paducah and every so often Decatur. It's been sixteen years now, and no one's tumbled to it. The only thing that changed was when the owner wanted to establish a presence down here and tapped me for that. Now I mostly make legit deliveries for his firm all over this area, and only every so often a drug run. The guy's a genius!"

The man seemed finished, and Father John spoke up. "What made you decide to confess now? I mean, it's been so long. Why now?"

Before the man could answer, the phone rang. Father John was secretly relieved. He had grown increasingly tense, perhaps visibly, for all he knew. He excused himself to answer the phone in the next room, explaining that he would need privacy, if it were the call he had been expecting. "I hope you don't mind. It should only take a moment. It's very important." The man gave him a strange look but didn't object.

It took, indeed, only a few minutes, but it wasn't the call he had anticipated. Instead, it was Vera Lansing, an old, lovable but very eccentric widow, one of his beloved St. Helena's cat-lickers. Father John realized instantly she would ask about the Mass for her husband that was scheduled several weeks hence, and he knew this wouldn't be the last such call before that day, either. Vera's memory wasn't the best anymore, but perhaps it was rather that, with lots of time on her hands, she simply wanted to connect with someone for a few minutes. *Goodness knows she misses her husband!*

"How are you Vera?" He cut right to the chase: "Wondering about your Ned's Mass?"

Of course!

"It's three Wednesdays from now. Don't fret! I haven't forgotten."

She wouldn't fret, but it took her several minutes to say so.

On the outside chance that she was merely lonely, Father John always took time to chat with her, just as he would several more times before that Wednesday, and just as he would for even longer conversations after that – whenever she might call.

He always reminded himself to get her last name correct. He had nicknamed her Mrs. Gensing and would be mortified if he ever actually said that to her face. One of her many eccentricities was an obsession with herbal remedies. Few Southern Illinois natives identify with that, so she certainly stood out. Thus far, despite her persistence, he had been able to blunt her attempts to have him sample her wares. And so far he'd avoided using that nickname in her hearing.

He hung up, took a deep breath and went back to the confession.

# CHAPTER XVII

Upon re-entering the room, the priest was surprised to see his visitor standing, apparently pacing the floor. "You all right?" he asked.

"Did you tell someone about my confession just now?"

"Of course not," Father John said, looking genuinely troubled. "I thought you understood that. That's one of the most sacred of trusts. It's just something a priest wouldn't do!"

"You were gone a while – long enough to make a phone call."

"Well, I didn't," the priest said with a touch of indignation. "That was an old lady with little else to do than worry about when I'm going to offer Mass for her deceased husband. People like that need some conversation, you know. But it wasn't the call I was expecting. That one could still come any time now." He eyed the man carefully. "If it makes you nervous, I just won't take any more calls until we've finished."

"I'd appreciate that," the man said with a touch of sarcasm.

"So be it, then," Father John said, calm returning to his voice. "Now, where were we? Oh, yes. You didn't have a chance to tell me why you're confessing this after all these years."

"I'd rather finish my story, okay?"

The priest nodded. He had thought the man was through. *There's more?*

"Things were great 'til that skeleton was found. Even that wasn't so bad. But then those guys blabbed to the sheriff. Lucky I decided to eat at the truck stop the morning they planned that – God only knows where this might have gone otherwise! There's no statute of limitations on murder, you know.

"Maybe I panicked, I'm not sure. They may never figure out exactly how the guy died, let alone who did it or even who he was, since all they've got's a skeleton. My boss was clever giving me those chemicals! But they can still use dental records! And who knows? Maybe they'd find out his identity and somehow trace it all to me. I figured I couldn't chance that. So I decided to send a message or two. Looking back, *maybe* I could've just took my chances …

"Well, anyway, I decided to slash the tires of the two guys on my block … "

Father John couldn't help himself and broke in. He had already figured out that he was talking to Gilbert Wetzel, Rick and Harry's Ash Street neighbor. But he didn't let on and coyly asked: "But why'd you slash a tire on that third car?"

"To throw everyone off, of course," the man said, sounding a touch superior. Then he looked quizzically at the priest. "You don't know who I am, do you?" When the priest didn't answer, he continued: "I'm Gil Wetzel – their neighbor. I think you'll have to admit that doing my own tire was pretty clever!"

"Why leave the knife then? That doesn't sound so clever."

Father John realized that he might have sounded combative. But Gilbert answered him evenly, apparently taking the question at face value. "I heard a noise and figured I'd best get outta there pronto. I bolted and, in my haste, I left the knife. I regretted that later, of course, but I was at least glad I decided to wear gloves. No fingerprints! I just had to hope they'd never be able to trace the knife."

Now that the man's identity was out in the open, Father John was emboldened to ask: "So you overheard them in the restaurant?"

"Right. And they haven't clue one it was me that did. I helped Harry with his car the other day and figured that out."

"Was it you who went after Willy Peters too?"

"Yeah."

"Why? How is any of that keeping your secret safe?" Father John asked, genuinely puzzled.

"Well, one thing's kind of led to another. Things are in motion now."

Father John looked puzzled. He didn't understand that logic. But when his penitent didn't offer anything further, he debated about filling the silence with the mention of Jim and Pete and their wrecks. He changed the subject instead. "Well, then, is there anything else you wish to confess?"

"I don't think so, no."

"So, can you tell me now why you decided to make a confession after all this time?"

"Well, as I said, I wasn't sorry for killing him … "

"At the time, you mean?"

"Right."

"But you are now, is that it?"

"No … "

"Excuse me," Father John said. "I'm confused. If you're not sorry now, why are you confessing?"

"Well, he deserved it, you know. I don't think … "

"I'm not sure anyone deserves to be murdered, Mr. Wetzel," Father John said softly. "Not even molesters. *Or* people who talk to sheriffs," he added even more quietly. He wondered later if Wetzel even heard that last part.

"Well, he did deserve it. And I'm not sorry – not then, not now!"

"But do you understand that I cannot offer you absolution if you aren't sorry? You have to be sorry to receive forgiveness."

For the first time Gil Wetzel's face evidenced some confusion, some loss of confidence. He took his time processing this new information. "But you have to forgive me," he finally blurted out.

"I'm sorry," Father John said slowly and softly, "but I can't."

"You have to! That's the whole point!"

"The whole point?"

"Yes. You have to forgive me. You have to! I need your silence!" He was almost shouting now.

"My silence?"

"Yes. Your silence! I need your silence. You have to be silenced!"

Father John didn't understand and finally said as much.

"Don't you get it? I can't have you meddling!"

"Meddling?"

"Yeah. I know you've been talking to those guys. Harry said so. You're as dangerous to me as they are. Maybe more."

It was clearly not beneath Gil Wetzel to put the priest's life in jeopardy. When Father John finally spoke, however, it wasn't out of self-concern, but for theological accuracy. "Do you think that if I give you absolution, I won't be able to talk about what you've said, and you'll be safe from my 'meddling?'"

"Yeah."

"And if I don't give your absolution, you won't be protected?"

"Right."

"Well, you may not realize it, but you've already tied my hands."

The man just stared at him.

"Once a confession is begun – or anything that even looks the least bit like one – they call that a 'putative confession' in church jargon, a presumed confession, if you will – as soon as something like that begins, the seal of confession kicks in. I'm not allowed to speak about this matter, even if there's no forgiveness offered when we're finished. If it's 'safe' you're wanting, you've already got it!"

The man's face slowly relaxed but then tensed up again. "How can I believe that's true?"

"You want to see it in a moral theology text or a copy of Canon Law?"

"What are those things?"

"Moral theology's the study of right and wrong. The rules, if you want, for living a moral life. And since confession deals with that, the seal of confession's in there too. Canon Law is church law.

The laws or rules are all listed in a book – nearly a couple thousand, actually."

The man's face remained screwed up.

"Or check with another priest! Call one now. You do all the talking, so I can't possibly prompt him. You'll see that what I'm saying is true."

"I could trust that!"

"Better still, do you want to call the chancery office?"

"The what office?

"Chancery! It's where the bishop works, and all the officials of the diocese too. Any of those priests could tell you."

"Sounds even better. What's that number?"

Gil Wetzel was soon talking to the diocesan chancellor, who in short order confirmed what Father John had said. Relieved, Gil put the phone down. "I guess you're right. I feel better now."

But Father John was not about to lose a penitent if he could help it. "Are you sure you're not sorry, Mr. Wetzel?" he asked quietly.

"Absolutely sure. And all the stuff I've done … I'm prepared to do more, if I have to. No one's gonna jail me for offing that pervert!"

"Can I persuade you, at least, not to do *anything else* you may regret. As I said, are you sure these things are helping you, are really protecting your secret? Seems to me they aren't and, worse, could get you caught. God knows, they're surely not good for those young men who, after all, merely said they noticed a funny smell in the woods."

"Don't care what you say. Things are in motion now. And it's every man for himself!" Gil Wetzel was getting visibly worked up.

Puzzled again by that logic, Father John nonetheless had the presence of mind to softly and very genuinely say: "I can't, of course, force you, Mr. Wetzel. But please know that when you change your mind – notice I said 'when', not 'if' – I'll gladly offer you God's and the church's forgiveness."

His angry look remained, and the priest gently added: "I truly mean that."

"Whatever! I got what I came for. Thank you very much," he said sarcastically and abruptly stood up. Without another word, he opened the door, made his way into the lobby and out of the rectory.

*What in heaven's name now? And to think I was beginning to feel honored to hear that confession!*

# CHAPTER XVIII

Father John watched Wetzel from the front door, hoping that he would think better and come back. But when his car disappeared and didn't return, Father John reluctantly closed the door and went to his desk to ponder his situation.

*I've been had – plain and simple – and I'm as much a victim of a warped but clever conspiracy as Jim and Willy and poor Pete. Wetzel is clever, all right! Isn't there anything I can do?*

He knew the answer in his heart of hearts: There was nothing he could do. His hands were tied, his lips sealed. He couldn't let on that he had seen the man or even knew him, for, truth to tell, he had never met him before that very day. It dawned on Father John that he *had* seen him at the funeral Mass. He remembered registering the face but not knowing its identity. Wetzel hadn't been at the wake or the cemetery, as far as Father John knew. He must be from out of town, he had concluded at church. Then he realized that funeral parlor and cemetery were settings that were too intimate. He could be recognized at those places, and were he to be questioned about his presence, probably wouldn't have good answers – whereas, the church could provide anonymity.

*Even so, what good could be served by being at the church? The man's logic defies me! Perhaps it's a way of keeping tabs on the young men, checking them out for clues to serve for future torture. Good grief, John, you're becoming as warped as he is!*

He sat morosely, realizing more and more just how hamstrung he was. He couldn't advise Pete's friends now or even tell them why.

It dawned on him that he would have to be evasive with them … and with the sheriff. *This is awful!*

He recalled his seminary days – so many years ago now – when the moral theology prof had led them through various scenarios involving the seal of confession. One, in particular, involved a penitent who had poisoned the altar wine. Did the priest have to drink it? Yes, they had been told. It had seemed so far-fetched, even laughable. Yet he was now involved in something hardly far-fetched and certainly not funny. He was drinking *someone else's* poison, it seemed. An intolerable, scary and even demonic bind to find oneself in. He had absolutely no idea how to deal with the sheriff – or the young men.

He was beginning to feel literally sick to his stomach, when the phone rang. It was his friend, Fr. Harold Fick.

"Harold! Hola! Where've you been? Haven't seen you in weeks." He was brightening up as he listened intently to his friend talk.

"Well, yes, I suppose early wild flowers *are* in bloom now, and it *would be* nice to see them. But do we have to drive all the way to Peoria?" More listening!

It occurred to him, as Harold chattered on, that this trip might be a way to avoid the sheriff and the young men for at least a few days. Then he felt guilty. But Harold kept talking, and the longer he did, the more the idea appealed to him.

"Okay, okay. You've convinced me. When would you like to leave?"

He listened briefly. "I suppose I can be ready by 9 or so tomorrow. I'll have finished Mass. And I've got today to take care of some things. You sure we'll be back Saturday? Good, then. Tomorrow!"

He hung up, already calculating whom to call and what to tell them. He would cancel the other morning Masses with an announcement tomorrow. And he would let his secretary know. *That's one call.* He would call the sheriff and, with any luck, just leave a message. *And I think I'll call Paul. He'll be at work, but he has a message machine – even better!*

It was falling into place. Besides, driving could provide time for mulling things over. Perhaps some new wrinkles would emerge. *Maybe my style won't be cramped as much as I fear!*

The calls were easily placed. His desk was next. A couple of hours later, backlogs were relatively erased, piles shaved down, even next Sunday's sermon started. He would have to work on it while he was away, of course, but that shouldn't be a huge problem. He went next to his bedroom to pack. By supper, all seemed in order. No calls had come in all day long. He just hoped his luck would hold out that evening.

In the morning, he felt rested and eager and was surprised at having slept so well. He had thought his situation would keep him tossing and turning all night, but that didn't happen.

He was chomping at the bit when Harold arrived shortly after 9. With Harold driving, he could finally relax when the Algoma city limits sign appeared in the passenger-side mirror of his friend's blue

Buick. He just hoped that things would work as smoothly for the sheriff and the young men while he was gone.

# CHAPTER XIX

They stayed with Harold's friend in a parish on Peoria's north side and took day trips throughout the countryside to see the flowers, occasionally stopping to wander through areas where the blooms were more abundant. The spring weather was thoroughly cooperative, warm and balmy, with absolutely clear and gorgeous skies. Once they ate lunch in a casino, where Harold won $23 on a penny slot machine. John had sipped a diet cola and watched, enjoying Harold's lucky streak as much as the man himself.

One nice thing about getting away with just priests, he knew, was that they could drop the formalities. It was "Harold" and "John" for those few days, and "Bob" when they were with Harold's friend in the evenings. He was the pastor of the relatively small parish where they stayed. It was thoroughly relaxing and without interruptions, even though John had left a note saying where he would be. Saturday morning came, in many ways, too soon.

The return trip deliberately avoided the interstates and allowed the priests to glimpse more wild flowers from their car. John looked over his sermon one last time, promising not to bother Harold with it. Harold insisted on hearing it, however, in hopes that it might provide something to add to his own sermon. Afterward, he thanked John but said that, while he liked it, it was totally different from his.

When Harold dropped him at St. Helena's, the tower clock was sounding half past 1. He had time to get ready for confessions and Mass, even to glance at mail and messages. There was nothing from either the sheriff or the young men, thank goodness. He got back into his "Father John" mode and went over to church a few minutes before confessions were to begin. Just two penitents were awaiting him.

None of the young men attended the Saturday evening Mass, and he put off contacting them or the sheriff. He would probably see the entire skeleton crew the next morning. Time enough to begin his evasions! He had thought about his situation the past few days and decided that it may not be as difficult as first feared. He could say that he knew nothing more when asked by any of them. The sheriff would be another matter entirely. That he would have to play by ear.

All six remaining members of the skeleton crew were at Sunday's Mass. He had begun to mentally call them by that title but wasn't sure he could say it to their faces yet. They were sitting in their usual places around the church and looked calm enough. After Mass, they came to him in a group.

"Hope you had a nice time away, Father," Jim said. "We had a relatively quiet time here ourselves, but I can't say it was exactly calm for any of us."

"Did something happen?" Father John asked.

"No. It's just that we're all on edge since Pete died," Tom said. He glanced around at the others nodding in agreement.

"Are your families okay? I assume they're out of town, as the sheriff suggested."

"They're all away, yes. We're off in different directions to see them today, as a matter of fact. But they seem fine," Jim said.

"Be sure to have things secure at your homes. Are your neighbors helping watch things in your neighborhoods?"

"Yes, we've taken care of that, and they've been glad to help."

"I hope you didn't have to tell them the whole story."

"Well, only two of us live in the same neighborhood. So far, we've been able to pretty much say our wives and kids are visiting Grandma and Grandpa. If things don't come off center soon, we'll have to come up with other stories, I suppose," Tom said.

"Well, have a nice time with your families today, anyway," Father John said. "I hope you know you're still all in my prayers."

"We do," several said simultaneously.

"Before we get out of here, though, Father … " It was Harry. "You spoke of praying for us. Have you got a book that might help me pray better? I recently found the need for that," he said and smiled.

"I think I can find one. Want to wait a moment or two? I have to say goodbye to some people and lock up. Then I can dig it out for you."

"Sorry, but I can't wait. And I don't know what time I'll be back tonight. Can you drop it by tomorrow night after work?"

"Sure. Who knows? It might take a while to find it, anyway. Be glad to stop by tomorrow evening. 6?"

"Good enough. I should be home by then. On second thought, make it a little later. Okay?"

"Sure 'nuff. See you then." He waved goodbye to them all and turned to search out other parishioners.

The rest of the day was spent plowing through mail and clearing off his desk. After putting aside the book, plus a pamphlet, for Harry, he was tempted to call the sheriff, but decided otherwise. It was probably his day off, and not calling gave him another evasion-free day.

Late the next morning, he wandered uptown in search of news. The Becker Pharmacy was his first stop. Fred greeted him cheerily from behind the prescription counter. "Hey, where you been? Haven't seen you all last week."

"Went to Peoria with Fr. Fick. It was a nice getaway. But here I am, and I'm starved for news! Anything happen while I was gone?"

"Can't say as there's been that much." Fred said. "Let me finish this prescription. The lady'll be here for it soon."

"Where's Frieda?" He hadn't realized until just then that she was nowhere to be seen. There was, in fact, no one else in the store.

"Got a nasty summer cold. I put her to bed, despite the fact that if she were here spreading germs, we might make a bit more money," he said and grinned ear to ear.

"Sorry to hear about her. Is something going around? Should I be taking precautions?"

"Nah. She's the only one I'm aware of. Just a fluke – maybe even allergies."

Father John busied himself at the greeting-card rack until Fred could step out from behind his counter. As he finally approached the priest, the pharmacist asked: "Want something to drink?"

"No, thanks. Just came by to chat. Got time?"

"I do, now that I've finished that prescription. Sit a spell." He beckoned to a booth, and both men eased themselves into it. Fred was carrying his portable phone, just in case.

"Wasn't that sad about young Pete Hamilton?" the pharmacist asked. "Such a nice young man."

"Yes, and it didn't help any that he's an only son. Thank goodness there are two daughters! They all took it hard – especially Pete's sisters," Father John said, his eyes watching Fred carefully to see what more he might know about Pete's death. When the pharmacist let the matter drop without further comment, the priest was satisfied that the sheriff had kept a lid on that. He felt relieved.

"So, nothing really popping this past week? It was a dumb-luck good time to be away, I suppose," Father John said with a shy smile.

"Well, when does anything really exciting happen in this town in summertime, anyway?" Fred said, rather seriously. He loved to be able to pass on tidbits of information, and whenever there were few such to pass on, he acted like he felt cheated by fate.

"Now, now," Father John said in mock seriousness. "You'll get your chances soon enough." He was trying to lighten the conversation, but realized that was probably truer than he would like it to be.

"The Methodist pastor is up for review again. But no big deal. It's routine. Shouldn't amount to his being replaced or anything."

"That's one less bureaucratic thing we priests have to deal with. Though, having a bishop who does essentially the same thing's bad enough! And he doesn't even put that on a timetable!" Father

John was almost laughing and hoped that Fred realized he was kidding. It had become standard fare between them: One would cast aspersions on the powers-that-be of some institution, and the other would come to the defense of the maligned authority figure. This time, however, Fred merely grinned, tacitly agreeing with his friend.

"So," Father John added, "I assume you don't think I need to send him condolences or anything."

"Might be funny if you did," Fred suggested.

"Maybe I'll take him to breakfast and put him on about it. I could do that this week," Father John said, warming to the idea. He made a mental note to call the minister.

"Heard anything further about that skeleton, Father?"

"Have you?" Father John said, without giving a real answer.

"Nope. I think that's a dead issue, if you'll pardon the pun," Fred said with a silly grin.

"Oh, I imagine *something* will be said eventually," Father John said, truthfully enough.

"Yeah, I guess. But it sure doesn't seem to be the big story everyone thought it would be. I suppose I can wait to hear."

"Guess I'll be moseying on," Father John said, rising from the booth. "The older I get, the harder these booths are to negotiate, Fred."

"Tell me about it," the pharmacist said. "But, as much as I stand all day, it's nice to sit every so often. Don't stop coming now!"

"It's a deal. Maybe next time I'll even have a little ice cream. Although my doctor thinks I should lose some more weight."

"Haven't you shed a few pounds lately?"

"Yes, thanks to Lent. And I've kept them off, too. But, you know, if I get in to see Doc Wilson soon, perhaps I can sit up and take some ice cream nourishment after that," he said and winked. "I think I *am* going to take that minister to breakfast!" He waved goodbye and left.

As he walked, he began to ruminate. *Against my better judgment, I'd better see the sheriff. I'll have to eventually, and it might as well be now. Maybe he's cracked the case, and I'll be off the confessional hook!*

He headed toward the courthouse and ducked into the bank to deposit the Sunday collection. He had been walking around with over a thousand dollars in bills and checks – coins were always left in the rectory safe until they accumulated and could be brought to the drive-up facility. He hadn't thought twice about carrying that kind of money around town before, but it struck him as he entered the bank that, with the likes of Gil Wetzel around, doing that might not be smart any longer. The thought wasn't entirely rational, but he would still have to think about it. He didn't say hello to Bobbie Sue or Bob Lanner, and with Maisie absent on Mondays, he simply made the deposit and left.

He crossed the street toward the jail on the other side of the courthouse. He asked to see the sheriff only to be told that "the boss" was out of town. "He's in Springfield for the day, Father."

That was more than he thought prudent for the deputy to share with just anyone. *Maybe that's just because I know the sheriff's in cahoots with the state police over his deputy. But then, perhaps the officer gave it out because he's seen me here talking with the sheriff.*

He thanked the man and asked that the sheriff be told that he had stopped. On his leisurely walk back to St. Helena's, he felt some relief at not yet having to be evasive with Lawrence Toler, whom he had come to consider a friend, even though their connections since last summer were only professional. But he still couldn't bring himself to call him Lawrence to his face, let alone Larry. It was always "Sheriff Toler." *But then, he only calls me* Father John.

He spent the afternoon reading, a rare privilege. There was seldom time for that. After a light supper, he drove to Harry's home with the reading material he had dredged up for him. He arrived twenty minutes after the hour to find Harry just getting out of his car.

"How's this for timing?" he said, climbing out of his black Taurus.

"Not bad. You been driving around here just so's you could make a dramatic entrance?" Harry said, grinning.

"Right. Nothing if not dramatic – that's me!"

"Whatcha got for me, Father?"

"These might help. Glad you're showing an interest in prayer these days, but sorry it's taken this sort of thing to bring that about."

"Hope I'm not being lulled into a false sense of security. I actually didn't feel any tension today. But I'll still use what you've brought."

"Good. If there are questions about prayer or these two pieces, feel free to give me a buzz."

"Will do." Then, looking beyond Father John, he added: "You ever met Gil Wetzel? Or do you even want to?"

“Why do you ask? It hadn’t occurred to me … ” Father John began, nervously realizing that he had better be careful of his words.

“There he is, just getting out of his truck.”

“No need to meet him. Thanks, anyway.” But, encouraged by Harry’s gesture, he turned to look in the direction of Harry’s glance. It was Wetzel, sure enough. Father John tried not to register any telling look on his face and turned back to Harry.

“Must’ve gone to the store for groceries just now. He told me this morning that it was good to get home after a week away.”

Father John said goodbye, but as he turned to go, he realized that something wasn’t quite right with Harry’s statement. He turned back to ask: “What did he tell you?”

“That he was gone over a week? That?”

“That’s what I thought you said. But I don’t think that’s right.”

“What makes you say that? You don’t even know him, Father.”

“You’re right, but I saw his face at Pete’s funeral. I remember not knowing who he was and figured he must be an out-of-town friend, since he wasn’t sitting with the family. You sure you heard him right? Maybe he just forgot.”

“I’m sure I heard right. And I don’t think he forgot because he asked if anything important happened while he was gone. When I mentioned Pete’s funeral, he sure acted like it was news to him.”

“That’s strange!” Father John was elated at the turn of events.

“Sure is. What you make of it?” Harry looked genuinely puzzled.

"Don't know. Why would he cover up being at the funeral?" Father John mused, coyly.

"Well, I'm paranoid enough to tell the sheriff about it. I don't trust anyone anymore!" Harry sounded very serious.

"Perhaps not a bad idea! Gonna give him a call?"

"I think so."

"I tried to see him this morning, but he was in Springfield. He might be back now, though. Anyway, good luck." He tried to sound nonchalant.

"Will do, Father. Might even call you after I finish talking to him."

"I'll be at home."

Father John went to his car and pointed it back toward St. Helena's. He could hardly contain himself and plunked down beside the phone as soon as he got back inside the rectory.

# CHAPTER XX

It wasn't long before Harry called. The sheriff was busy but would call back soon, and he would let Father John know what came of that. Fifteen minutes later, Harry's brief message was that the sheriff seemed interested and would look into things in the morning. Father John thanked the young man and wished him pleasant dreams. But when he put the receiver back onto the cradle, he was almost certain that he would soon hear from the sheriff. He wasn't disappointed.

He was tempted to answer the phone "Hello, Sheriff," but resisted the urge.

"You must know Harry Grant called me," the lawman began.

"I told him to."

"What do you make of that stuff about his neighbor?"

"That he claimed to be away, whereas I saw him at the funeral?"

"Yes."

"Whatever it means, it isn't that he forgot. Sounds deliberate to me, and he had to know it wasn't true. But what do you think?"

"I think I agree with that. Sounds like a lie."

"So what about that, Sheriff?" Father John was careful to cross no moral or ethical lines.

"Harry mentioned paranoia. That's not unreasonable. But I can't imagine why he should *literally* be afraid of his neighbor. After all, Wetzel had his own tire slashed," the lawman said.

"Yes, but we weren't certain what that meant, as I recall," Father John countered. "The slasher could've been unsure whose cars were whose. And one of us figured it might even have been deliberate to throw off suspicion. In any event, I guess I do agree: It *looks like* he's an innocent victim." Father John chose his words carefully to appear objective and allow the sheriff to draw his own conclusions.

"Yes, but Wetzel's acting strange, and I'm inclined to dig deeper. What do we really know about the man, anyway?"

"That a rhetorical question, Sheriff?"

"Yes. I was about to say that we know he originates elsewhere – up north, I think. And he's a trucker. And, oh yes, he has a well-known temper. Not much else. None of that generates suspicion. But I'm uneasy about that lie – and that's what we should call it now, a lie."

"So, what now?"

"Think I'll get the state police on him too. I was in Springfield today at a sheriffs' gathering. But I also checked in with those guys. Hank's phone records show nothing, but he does have elevated income levels. No paper trail, though – cash, apparently. He may be moonlighting on security. I'm not sure he has time for that, but it *could* be. I'll have to nose that out on my own."

"What will checking on Wetzel prove?"

"Not sure, but who knows what we might find. I *think* we can look. I'll ask Hugh Monroe. Gotta get me a warrant first."

"Good luck! And thanks again for including me."

"No. *Thank you* for sending Harry my way. I'll be in touch. Night!"

"Good night, Sheriff."

Father John was hoping against hope that something would come of this. What or how was beyond him, but he could hope.

*Shades of my funeral homily!*

# CHAPTER XXI

Priests rarely welcome meetings or think of them as diversions from anything. They're often just nuisances. People in other professions might view them similarly, for all Fr. John knew, but he certainly knew how priests felt. Even so, Father John awoke the next morning to the realization that the deanery meeting could well serve to provide just that for him: a welcome diversion from the stress he was feeling over keeping the seal of confession inviolate.

Deanery meetings are gatherings of priests and sometimes other pastoral ministers in an area determined not so much by geography as by overall number of parishes. In Southern Illinois, single counties rarely constitute deaneries, Clinton County being a notable exception. Belleville, along with a few parishes outside the city, comprises a deanery. The same is true for East St. Louis and environs. But in the southeastern section of the diocese, where parishes are scattered over a broader area and there are only handfuls of Catholics, the deanery is spread over many counties. Numbers of priests attending deanery meetings, therefore, can range from ten to thirty or more. And while such gatherings, in theory, facilitate cooperation among priests and parishes on a regional basis, in practice they give priests a chance to socialize and often accomplish little else. While Father John usually treated such moments as intrusions, today's meeting was one of those rare times when he looked forward to getting away for the better part of the day.

The meeting itself was hardly inspiring. But it was the diversion he had hoped for, and for that he was grateful. The fellowship was also welcome. As he renewed old ties and swapped stories, he felt a release from the tension that had been building up. More precisely, he didn't notice the tension at all. On the drive back to Algoma, however, he felt its return and, reminding himself to be positive, thanked God for the brief relief and tried to concentrate on the lovely spring countryside all around him. The greens were vibrant in the late-afternoon light, the vegetation lush, and the crops brimming with spring promise. *What a wonderfully productive area of the world you live in, John! Rejoice in it!*

He was usually joyful. But that day, and for some days now, he had found himself negatively preoccupied with … what? *Fear? Loathing? That's too strong a face for it – but something like that.*

The ominous conspiracy threatening the young men had overtaken him gradually, he realized, finally to crash in on his consciousness with that trucker's confession. Thinking now of Gilbert Wetzel, his mind turned to sheriff Toler. *I hope he can find something to link that guy to everything.* But, in his heart of hearts, he had his doubts. It seemed such a stretch, such an uphill battle and much too dependent on serendipity. *Hope, John! Hope!*

His brief moments of respite well behind him by the time he opened his rectory door, he was greeted by several messages on his answering machine. One of them, the voice of sheriff Toler, caught his attention. "Call me ASAP."

He vetoed driving to the jail and picked up the phone instead to save time. He had to wait several minutes, but the sheriff finally came on. "Father John! Glad you called. I've got interesting news."

"Don't keep me in suspense."

"Good news all right, but it requires some explaining. The state has computers for this sort of thing, but if one of their boys didn't have a memory for details, they wouldn't have even used them to run this down. They didn't find anything in the phone records of my deputy for the past year, so they went back several years and still didn't find anything. But now they've started in on Wetzel. He makes good money, but it all comes from his trucking firm. So the financial probe hasn't yielded anything on him, at least not yet. Nor have his phone records.

"But that's where the guy's memory comes in. Wetzel puts a lot of calls in to his company in a Chicago suburb and to his boss' home. No surprise there. But the sergeant in Springfield thought he'd seen that home number in Hank's file. Sure enough! There it was in Hank's incoming calls from a couple of years back! Bingo!"

"Am I hearing you right, Sheriff? Wetzel's boss called Hank?"

"Right."

"How many times?"

"Only once – but right before Hank's income started to rise!"

"You think he's in the pay of Wetzel's boss?"

"Good guess. It's flimsy. Only one call! But there's no reason for that one call. And right then Hank starts gettin' more cash! I think we got ourselves something."

"But what's that got to do with the skeleton or the young men?"

"Don't know. But we're sure gonna find out!"

Father John was intrigued. This didn't implicate Wetzel, though it points to Wetzel's boss, who, after all, was part of the original murder, as Father John knew.

"What next?"

"I think we got probable cause to get tough with Hank now. I'm checking with Judge Monroe before I do anything else. But I can spin a few webs here. I think Hank's been brought in for protection. You know, a police insider to stay on top of anything that might be threatening some bad guy or other – maybe Wetzel, though if so, we still have to find out what he's up to. At least, that's my first guess. As I said, I'll be talking to Hugh Monroe. I'm waiting for him to call, as we speak. Thought you'd want to know."

"Thanks. You know I do. And will you also let me know what develops from this?"

"I will. Later!"

Father John sat thinking by the phone, ignoring his other messages. *What in heaven's name does this have to do with that murder? If Hank's involved in anything, it's way too recent to have helped with the skeleton guy. And Wetzel didn't speak of that, either. In fact, he never even mentioned Hank. This doesn't make much sense – unless Hank really is some sort of insurance policy, maybe for the drug stuff. I hope the sheriff can handle this and still get Wetzel for that murder ... not to mention all this recent stuff!* He said a silent prayer.

There was another call from the jail twenty minutes later. Judge Monroe agreed that they should look into the deputy. Things were beginning to sizzle.

# CHAPTER XXII

Maisie Brown called the next morning to switch cleaning days. She came every other Tuesday, but that wouldn't be convenient for next week, she said. Father John talked with her for a time, all the while worrying that, with the line tied up, he couldn't get a call from the sheriff. After he hung up, he realized how silly a worry that was. It was probably too soon for the sheriff to know more about his deputy, and he would call once the line was open, anyway.

He frittered away the rest of the morning on busywork, filing sermon notes and generally trying to just stay occupied in a useful fashion. But by the end of the morning, he was in a state. It was all he could do to keep from bothering the sheriff until after lunch.

But the sheriff beat him to the punch. At ten minutes past noon, he phoned. "Father John?"

"Hello, Sheriff. So glad it's you. I've been itchy."

"Well, I tell you … if this don't beat all! My deputy is stonewalling. He knows I don't have enough to arrest him, and he refuses to say much of anything. Just flat out refuses. It's like he's taking the Fifth. I told him our relationship is near to breaking. Didn't seem to matter! So I finally told him I'd put him on administrative leave if he didn't come across. I gave him the lunch hour to think. If he's still uncooperative, I may even give him 'til tomorrow, but no longer'n that! He's hiding somethin', and I'm going to get it out of him!"

Usually a calm man, the sheriff was angrier than Father John had ever known him to be. "You keeping your professional cool?"

"Yeah, but you're hearing what I'm really feeling, Father."

"That's fine. You can let it all out with me any time you like. Just be careful to rein it in around him."

"I know. I know."

"Want some lunch? Maybe that'll help keep you calm."

"Can't. Sorry. Promised my wife I'd be home for a sandwich."

"Well, I'm on pins and needles too, Sheriff. Let me know if and when you get a breakthrough."

"I will. Bye."

Father John didn't expect to hear anything more that day from the sheriff and was surprised when he did around 2 that afternoon.

"You're not going to believe this," the lawman began. "He wants the FBI in on this, and refuses to say another word 'til they get here. Looks like that's what we'll be doing tomorrow: talking with the friggin' FBI – pardon my language, Father!"

"I thought you'd said they couldn't look into his records."

"That's right."

"And now he wants them in on this?"

"Right again."

"But they don't have jurisdiction, am I right?"

"I think you are. But it sounds like they know something. There's a call in to them now, and if they'll come, perhaps they do."

"And Hank knows about whatever that is?"

"Would seem so. I'm buffaloed. But I called – and we'll see."

"This is getting weirder and weirder. I hope they won't seal your lips such that you can't share it when you find out what's going on. I'm curious as the dickens," Father John said, genuinely excited.

"Oh, I'll let you know, all right – whatever I'm allowed to say. You can be sure of that, Father. You think *you're* curious!"

"When did you say this might happen?"

"I'm guessing not before tomorrow."

"Well, I'll be praying about it."

"Thanks."

"But before you hang up, has anything else been happening with the young men? I haven't heard from them … "

"Me, neither. Let's hope that end of things stays quiet."

"Ditto. Talk soon, I hope."

"Me too. Bye, Father."

Father John spent the rest of the day nervously puttering around. He couldn't find anything to occupy him in any satisfactory way, and whenever he stopped to think about anything other than the minutiae he was trying to bury himself in, his mind seemed to be thudding up against a brick wall. It was like looking at a whole lot of jigsaw puzzle pieces dumped on a table: no discernible theme – just an enormous task awaiting someone's very focused efforts.

By bedtime he was able to console himself with the realization that there hadn't been any distress calls from the skeleton crew. *Thank God for small favors!*

# CHAPTER XXIII

The parish secretary usually came in only on Monday, Wednesday and Thursday mornings. Father John took Mondays off, so he often saw her just after the Wednesday and Thursday Masses, which she attended routinely.

She greeted him cheerfully that Wednesday morning and handed him the mail from the parish post office box. Before he had gotten completely through it, the phone rang, and he soon heard her voice from the front office. "It's Mrs. Gensing."

He rose from his desk and went to her office, mostly to be sure she had muted the call before shouting to him. "She didn't hear that, did she?" he whispered with some concern.

"No. She's on hold."

"Good. I'm worried that she might overhear that sometime from you or me. I'd never be able to explain it. Probably shouldn't have shared that little joke with you. Sorry."

"Don't fret, Father. Your little secret's safe with me. I'll make sure she never hears that."

"Maybe we should both just not call her that," Father John mumbled as he returned to the phone in his office. He didn't see the broad smile on his secretary's face.

"Mrs. Lansing! How are you? Will you be able to attend your husband's Mass?"

The conversation seemed interminable, but he remained patient and breathed an audible sigh when he finally put the phone down. He could hear his secretary quietly giggling in the other room.

"Careful," he said, "or I may have you deal with her next time." It was an ongoing joke between them. He liked Betty, and often reminded himself how fortunate he was to have her – how fortunate the parish was. She had a level head, was polite and competent and possessed a sense of humor that had lifted his spirits more times than he could count. But that morning he reminded himself that, should the sheriff call while she was still there, he would take the call in his bedroom out of earshot.

Prompted by that thought, he shouted to her: "I should be getting an important call from sheriff Toler. Be sure to find me, if I have to wander away for any reason."

"Will do," Betty said.

He finished the mail but stayed at his desk, not wanting to miss that call. There were Communion calls to make, but he put them off. *I can do them this afternoon.*

But the call seemed destined not to come. Betty left at noon, and he wandered into the kitchen in search of a sandwich. He settled for the remains of a salad that should be eaten soon or thrown away, instead.

Lunch finished, and with still nothing from the jail, he reluctantly began to plan for the Communion calls, deciding which people to see today and which later. When the phone rang in the middle of that, he was certain it was the sheriff, but it was the chancery office instead. The Bishop's secretary wanted to be sure he had received a recent mailing. There had been a snafu, and she was checking. Since Father John didn't have e-mail, his name was on her to-call list.

"Yes, I got it, Shirley. Was something important omitted?"

"No, Father. The computer messed up the mailing list and some people didn't receive it. So far, five pastors need copies mailed to them. I'm glad you didn't get skipped."

"Thanks for checking, Shirley. Bye." He was always cordial with the chancery staff. Theirs is a thankless job, in his opinion, so he always went out of his way to be pleasant on the phone or when he saw them at their office. But he rarely held in high regard the mailings they sent out for the bishop and his staff. He would chuckle whenever he remembered what one of his cohorts had said about the volume of mail from that office. There was so much of it that the only good thing to do with it, the priest had said, was to bail it. "Amen" to that, in his opinion – and a good many other priests', as well.

Not only was there tons of mail, but most of it was of little importance and even less help. But, then, perhaps the bishop was simply accommodating a lot of people who thought their various programs were important enough to be seen by everyone. He never complained aloud, but chancery mail was one of his pet peeves.

The afternoon dragged on and he eventually went visiting the shut-ins. When he returned near suppertime, the phone machine's red light was blinking. Upset to have missed the sheriff's call, he checked the messages. There was just one. The sheriff was brief and to the point: "Phone me. You're not going to believe this!"

He hoped that he was still on duty. *I should put his number on speed dial. I phone it so often!*

"Yes, the sheriff's still here. May I tell him who's calling? Oh, yes, Father John. Just a moment."

"Father, I'd rather talk to you in person," the sheriff said when he came on the line. "I'm about to head home to supper, so I'll stop by, if that's all right."

"It's fine. Good news?"

"I'd say so, yes – but complicated. See you in a few minutes."

The few minutes stretched into twenty or more, and Father John realized that he was getting tense again. When the lanky lawman finally arrived, they sat in the kitchen, where the sheriff began telling Father John what he had learned from the FBI earlier that afternoon.

"You'll never guess why Hank's been acting so squirrelly, Father. The FBI has him doing an undercover thing!"

"What?"

"Hank's originally from up north. Perhaps you remember my telling you that. Well, even after all these years, his name somehow came up to the man in the Chicago area who happens to be Gil Wetzel's boss. He apparently thought Hank could be bought. He first contacted him nearly two years ago now. That was the phone number the state cop remembered in Hank's file. It was a one-time phone call, mind you. The idea was for Hank to be this guy's ace-in-the-hole, a mole in our department, to keep tabs on what we knew about his drug operation. You see, Wetzel's been running drugs for this guy probably since he got down here, and the FBI's on to it.

"Winstrom was supposed to provide the bad guys with insurance against getting caught – or at least give 'em a heads-up on whatever we might be up to down here. Only, Hank went right to the FBI."

Father John's face was showing surprise. He was pleased to have thought to register that emotion.

"The guy up north provided Hank a cell phone. The FBI knew about it, but we didn't, of course. The phone's registered to somebody else up north – not the drug guy. So we couldn't access any of that phone traffic when we went after Hank's info. Pretty clever, huh? And, they say, Wetzel's got one like it that he uses only for drug-related stuff. It's the only way he and Hank communicate, by the way. So the state didn't pick up on that, either.

"The FBI's been gathering information for way over a year now, to learn who else is involved besides Wetzel and his boss. Gradually they've gotten the other players who make the drug thing happen. And all the while, Hank's been working both sides of the fence but telling the FBI everything. And I mean *everything!*"

"But why weren't you told about this arrangement?"

"I asked the same question today. They didn't trust our little 'hick' department! I wasn't at all happy with that, and I told them so in no uncertain terms. They acknowledged that they might not have liked it either, if they were in my place. But they didn't apologize or back down. Hank, however, was apologetic as all get out, sayin' he wasn't allowed to put us in the loop. Hasn't been able to apologize enough, the poor guy!

"Well, he's been in thick with Wetzel all this while, you see, but they only communicate on cell phones, like I said. They're not even to be seen with each other. And since Wetzel's cell phone is also registered up north, we only got his home phone traffic.

"Hank's been aware of everything Gil's doing with the drugs, of course. But when the trucker started doing other stuff lately, he was puzzled, and he confronted him about it. You see, Gil's the person who's been harassing those young guys. And when Hank found out about that, he couldn't figure why he was doing it. Apparently it didn't come from the boss up north – it was Wetzel's idea solely.

"It came to a head the other day when Gil ran Pete off the road. Gil had Hank pick him up right after he set fire to the stolen car he used on Pete. Hank was pretty upset, but couldn't say that to Wetzel, of course. What he did say was that all the stuff he was doing could get everybody caught." Father John remembered saying as much to Wetzel, himself.

"But just here lately, Hank did tell the FBI that things were gettin' out of hand. And when Pete died, he nearly went ballistic. The FBI's been nearly ready to move on Wetzel and will be pulling Hank out of the operation when they do. But they can't do it just yet – not before making absolutely sure they can get the whole drug bunch, especially the boss. And that part still isn't quite ready.

"On top of everything, in the past couple of weeks, the feds told Hank to begin forcing Wetzel's hand by getting loose-lipped around town. That's when you and I started wondering about him. The purpose was to make things hotter for Wetzel. Hindsight says that it may not have worked quite that way. After all, Pete's dead … *although* they took pains to point out to me today, and especially to

Hank, that Hank's blabbing didn't cause that car incident, let alone Pete's death.

"Nonetheless, Hank's really bent out of shape. He feels they let things go on too long. And he really wants Wetzel brought down. He'd do it tonight if they'd let him. But the G-men want to do a sting, and we've all been told to hold our horses."

"But why's Wetzel bothering those young guys?" Father John sounded as sincere as he could.

"Oh, yeah. I forgot. Hank's not sure why the skeleton's so important to Wetzel or his boss – or maybe both – but he's guessing that they know about the guy's death. When the thing was found in the woods, and especially when the young guys talked, Wetzel got upset. Either the boss or Gil – doesn't much matter which, but it's probably Gil – decided on a rather systematic campaign of vengeance that seems to have escalated as it went along.

"Speaking of that, by the way, I've just ordered a much more thorough plan to protect those boys, I'm sure you'll be happy to know. I'm a little surprised one of them didn't call you about that." Father John shook his head to indicate that they hadn't.

"They all know about it, though I didn't tell 'em *why* I was doing it. I just said I decided on a 'better safe than sorry' strategy. There were no objections, to be sure, or questions about what prompted it, either. I also sort of let them know I'd be briefing you, so maybe that explains why they haven't called yet."

Father John had been mentally calculating that most of the bases were now covered. But since not everything about the skeleton was known yet, he decided to give that a nudge. *Careful now, John!*

"You think maybe the skeleton came from outside our area? I mean, you haven't found anyone missing from around here, right?"

"Yeah, it's probably not from here."

"Any idea where?"

"Well, Wetzel and his boss come from up around Chicago. Maybe the skeleton did too."

"Maybe," the priest said, privately relieved that the sheriff was finally getting on the right track.

"We can get the FBI to widen the search for us. All this investigating costs money. They can foot some of the bill." The sheriff smiled for the first time since he stepped into Father John's kitchen.

"But that won't be easy, I imagine. Chicago's a big place."

"Well, we can use dental records. That'll help some. And we'll look at records of missing persons from sixteen years ago. It's doable!"

"Good. Sounds like you're miles ahead of yesterday."

"We are. And I feel better about Hank, too. He's also relieved as well. I don't think he liked the rift growing between us any more than I did."

"I'm guessing you'll not be putting him on administrative leave," Father John said, smiling.

"Right. But he'll have to stay on that desk job a couple more days. The department knows the FBI was here today, and moving him now might raise too many questions. In a day or so, I'll say he's completed what I asked him to do, and he'll go back to regular duties. Of course, he'll still be a kind of double agent for the feds."

“Wow,” Father John said as he glanced at his watch. “Are you sure your wife is still waiting supper for you?”

“She knows something’s up. But that’s a good point. Unless there are urgent questions, I should be going. We can talk more tomorrow.”

“Should I call or wait to hear from you?”

“I’ll contact you. God only knows what might be going on by then! I think the FBI will be taking the lead now. So I’ll need to coordinate with them, and I have no idea what that might involve me in tomorrow!”

# CHAPTER XXIV

The next morning's Mass seemed somehow to have cleansed Father John's psyche. When he returned to the rectory for a little breakfast, the last thing on his mind was sheriff Toler or the skeleton crew – not even Gil Wetzel. He should have known better. He wasn't halfway through his small bowl of Cheerios when the phone rang.

"Hello," he said cheerily.

It was the jail. "Can you hold for the sheriff, Father?"

"Certainly," he said and carefully held the receiver away from his face while chomping down on the last bites of cereal from his bowl.

"Father John!" the sheriff said when he finally came on the line. "Things just won't settle down. Apparently Hank finally got through to the feds. They want him to convince Wetzel's boss to rein him in. I guess they got to thinking they couldn't sit around doing nothing with that wacko running around out of control."

"Sounds like good news, Sheriff."

"Maybe yes, maybe no. The problem is, how to do that. They're wanting Hank to phone the guy, but Hank seems to favor surprising him by showing up on his doorstep. Only, he doesn't know where he lives. All he's ever done is talk to him on that cell phone, and while he does that every so often, he's never met the guy. Doesn't even know the name of the suburb where he lives, let alone his address."

"So how can he just show up?"

"My point exactly. What Hank's leaning toward is to start driving and then call the guy when he gets north of Springfield – maybe even farther."

"What's wrong with that?"

"Well, the boss might not take kindly to it. It's pretty pushy, don't you think?"

"I don't know. What's pushy about it?"

"Well, here's an employee getting aggressive with his admittedly reclusive employer."

"Oh! I guess so. Anyway, anything decided on that?"

"They're still at it. But I called in case you had some ideas."

*Thanks a lot!* "Well, I don't really know. Let me think about it."

"You mean on the phone here, right? Because they're sittin' in my office right now discussin' it."

"You actually caught me finishing breakfast. Let me tidy up. I can think while I do that. I'll call you back in a few minutes."

"I suppose. As fast as you can, though, okay?"

"Right."

When he was finished, he still had no ideas but picked up the phone anyway.

"Sheriff, I'm drawing a blank."

"Well, they've decided anyway. He's going to drive up there, and when he phones the guy, he'll act a little stupid and say he just now realized he didn't know where the guy lives and take it from there. If he won't see him, Hank'll still get the message across that Wetzel needs to be controlled. If, on the other hand, he gets a face-to-face with the guy, it's possible he can learn more about him – and that's icing on the cake. The FBI puts that kind of information into the planning of a sting."

"You mentioned that before, a sting. What's that mean? I know what a sting is, but what exactly are they planning to do?"

"I don't think they know 'exactly' yet themselves, but they want to catch Mr. Big with some dope and, barring that, to somehow otherwise tie him to the whole operation. They haven't worked out all the details yet."

"So when's Hank leave?"

"He drove away just now. He's got two cell phones. He'll keep us up-to-date on the one and only use the other to talk to the boss."

"Sounds kind of cloak-and-dagger exciting."

"Maybe, unless you're Hank. But he actually seems pretty cool. I think he figures he's not in any real danger. The guy still thinks he's working for him, and all he's doing is the loyal thing: telling his boss about an unforeseen risk he needs to make a decision about."

"You think you'll have a better handle on it by tonight?"

"That's about right."

"Wish I could have been more help just now."

"No problem. Later!"

# CHAPTER XXV

The rest of Father John's day was to be spent on parish matters. He had the financial report to prepare for the parish council, and there were more Communion visits to do. He finished the finances, but there wasn't time to make the rounds of his final shut-ins before noon, so he grabbed two pairs of pants in need of mending and went in search of one of the town characters, Googie Gilden.

Small towns in Southern Illinois can be relied upon to have at least one seamstress to do the sewing that the average woman no longer seems to have the time, inclination or ability for. Algoma actually had several. But it also had one man: Googie Gilden.

A tailor for many years at a St. Louis department store before retiring, Googie had lived in Algoma since anyone could remember but originally hailed from somewhere out east. He had always been sketchy about that part of his life and his nickname's origin, as well. It had taken Father John more than five years to learn that the "G" by his name in the phone book actually stood for George, or maybe Georg.

Depending upon his mood, Googie would lead inquirers down a variety of garden paths. It was his long-dead wife's nickname when she wanted sex; or it was what they called him in the Garment District, to distinguish him from another George, whose last name began with "N" and was, therefore, called Noogie; or it was his handle in a gang of punks he had run with growing up in New York City. The list was endless. Whenever it came up, townsfolk could recite entirely different stories they'd been told. Googie was wonderfully creative. No one, not even Father John, was satisfied he'd heard the correct version. But it was fun trying to tease it out of the tailor, and that's what Father John suspected the game was all about: seeing how long the process could be prolonged and how much fun could be had.

The man was in his eighties and, as Father John anticipated, was to be found at home. So confident was Father John that he didn't phone ahead. The man's television was on full blast; Father John thought of entering without knocking because Googie might not hear him over the noise. But he knocked anyway – rather loudly, just in case. Googie appeared at the door in relatively short order.

He beamed when he saw the priest's face. "Come in, come in. I haven't seen you in too long. Would you like a beer?"

Father John grinned. He never knew what to expect from the elderly man. "I gave it up for Lent."

"Is it still Lent? I forget."

"No, but I keep it up because I lost a few pounds I don't want to see again." He remembered Doctor Wilson. *I've* got *to call the man!*

Spying the trousers in the priest's hands, he said: "So! You bring those because they don't fit any more?"

"No. Because they got ripped! Now that I've lost weight, they fit again! But I can't wear them with seats like these." He held them up to show the gaping hole where they had given way. They both laughed.

"I can fix them, but it'll cost an arm and a leg – and maybe a prayer too." He grinned.

"I can do the prayer right away. I may have to pay off the arm and leg on installments." It was Father John's turn to grin.

"Sit. Business is over. We can talk now. I'll call when they're ready. Not in a hurry, are you?" Father John shook his head and shrugged. "Good. Sit!"

Father John did as he was told. Googie went to his kitchen and returned with wine and glasses. "A little of this you can handle, no?"

"Okay. But only a little."

The wine poured, Googie looked over at the priest and said: "I hear you're involved in all this stuff with the young guys."

Father John almost dropped his glass. "Where'd you hear that? I thought you don't get around much these days. Didn't you complain to me last time, whenever that was – last fall – or longer – I can't remember? Didn't you complain, anyway, that you can't see to drive? I wondered about that, because you still do such good work on clothes."

"I have a magnifying glass for my work. And I imagine I said that because it's true. But I heard about you, nonetheless. I have my sources," he said with a sly grin.

"Guess so. I *am* involved, but it's because I'm their pastor."

"Not what I hear."

"So what do you hear?"

"That you've been talking to them *a lot*."

"That's somewhat true, but who'd you hear it from?"

"A trucker," he said, teasing him by drawing out the words.

*I'll bet I can guess who!* "You been eating at the truck stop? Thought you don't drive anymore."

"No, not at the truck stop, although I miss their food. You should take me there for breakfast some time."

"I could do that, but only if you tell me which trucker. I want to know who to watch myself around." He was trying to keep the banter light-hearted. But he was also getting more curious by the moment.

"A trucker who needed some work on his clothes."

"Figures! But you still haven't said who."

"Name's Wetzel. Not from around here originally … "

"You mean like you?" he was on a roll, and Googie was enjoying it.

"No, not like me. I've been here decades. This guy's new. Only came a few years back – less than twenty!"

"Just a kid, sounds like. Regular customer?"

"No. Even you come oftener!" Googie was getting into the game.

"Okay, you told me. When do you want to go to the truck stop?"

"How's tomorrow?" he said, grinning again.

"Too soon. I have to fast several days to avoid gaining back all that weight." Both men were grinning now. "But, if you twist my arm, I can get you right after tomorrow's Mass."

"Good. I'm glad you didn't try to convert me by saying I should go to your Mass."

"There's no hope for you. It's not that you're Jewish, Googie. It's that you don't go to church … synagogue."

"Where could I go to synagogue? The nearest one's in Belleville!"

"Centralia!"

"Used to be. It closed!"

"You sure?"

"I'm sure. I should know! Give me a break!"

"But you didn't even go there when it was open."

"Can't drive. Remember?"

"You got me. Maybe there's some exception for a Yiddisher like you. I don't know the Talmud well enough to be sure." Father John took another sip of wine. "This is good! Notice that I took the surprise out of my voice when I said that."

"It's expensive. I'm glad you only wanted a little."

The ease of their banter was a joy to Father John, and it had to also brightened Googie's day. But he was still wanting to find out exactly what Wetzel had said.

"So, tell me. Who's this Wetzel? And what'd he tattle about me?"

"He says he's met you."

"And that makes him an expert on what I do?"

"Maybe. Anyway, he says you're practically a rabbi to them."

"What? I read them the Torah?"

"Come on! You tell them what to do."

"You got the wrong guy. No one listens to me, especially young people." He was grinning, but he noticed that Googie wasn't.

"Not according to Wetzel! They hang on your every word."

"I don't know how he could know that. And they don't, I can tell you. You say he's met me?" Father John was hoping that Wetzel might have taken him off the hook by saying too much about the confession.

"So he says. You don't remember?"

"If he didn't introduce himself, how could I be sure? He isn't a member of our parish that I know of." *So far, so good, John!*

"I don't know if he did or not. But he knows you. So he says."

"Well, that's intriguing. Think I could convert him?" He was grinning again, and so was Googie.

"Always the converting. Get a life! But, anyway, those young guys! I think it's awful what's happening to them."

"Them? Pete Hamilton's the only one who's had something awful happen, dying in that wreck the other day. Terribly sad funeral!"

"Yes, but what about the window that got shot out? And that other wreck – who was it? Eisner – young Jim Eisner?"

"Yes, he had a wreck too, but he's okay. But you make it sound like fate is dealing those boys a deliberately bad hand."

"Wetzel thinks so."

"Really? Maybe he should talk to the police, if he thinks that."

"Well, what do I know? I'm just an old retired tailor who gets to eat at the truck stop tomorrow. Whoopee!"

Father John had finished his wine and took Googie's remark as a signal that their conversation was at an end. He stood up. Pointing to his pants, he said: "Think you'll have those done before Christmas?"

"If you're lucky. It won't be tomorrow! When you picking me up?"

"Right after Mass, like I said."

"So when's that? A Jew should know when you pray?"

"By 9. Don't give me trouble!" He smiled and stepped into the sunshine. From his car, he waved to the tailor still standing in his doorway.

*I like that man! But what's Wetzel up to, running at the mouth like that? Trying to get me to break the seal of confession?*

The afternoon was spent visiting the sick, and Father John went to bed early that night, surprised not to have heard from sheriff Toler. He hoped that wasn't a bad sign.

# CHAPTER XXVI

Meanwhile, Hank Winstrom had been making his way north and by early afternoon, when he got to the far side of Bloomington on I-55, decided that it was time to call the drug lord. He checked in with the sheriff and FBI guys for the go-ahead and then placed the call.

"This is Hank Winstrom."

"Yes?"

Their conversations had always been like that: business-like and no-nonsense. Hank always identified himself; the man never did.

"I have disturbing news."

The disembodied voice registered no alarm. "Go ahead."

"Wetzel's out of control. Are you aware of what he's been doing to the young guys who talked to the sheriff about a skeleton found in the woods recently?" There was a pause on the other end of the line, and Hank added: "You are aware of that skeleton, right?"

"Yes. Tell me more about what Wetzel's been up to."

"Well, I didn't know 'til lately that it was him doing it all, but those guys have been having things happen to them. One had a blowout, another's front window was shot out, and now one of them was run off the road and died. All these guys did was say they smelled something in the woods when they were kids. And it's Wetzel, all right, because he had me pick him up after he ran the guy off the road and then burnt the stolen car he used to do it. I told him all this stuff's pretty risky, but he's not listening."

More silence on the other end, so Hank continued. "I think this is so bad that I'm coming your way right now to talk about it." *Let's see what that provokes!*

No silence this time. "Not a good idea."

"To come to you or what Wetzel's doing?"

"Both."

"Well, I'm north of Bloomington already. I believe we need to think this through and I'd rather this way than by phone. I don't mind being your point man down south, but I don't want to be involved in anything like this. Wetzel's not acting responsibly, and I don't want to go down because of him. He could bring *everybody* down, you know."

"All right. Kankakee. Get off I-55 wherever you think best and come east. I'll see you at a small diner ten blocks off I-57 on the south side of the main drag. It's the only one in that block. Can't miss it. Be there by 3 and don't keep me waiting. Get something, if you're early. I'll have coffee when I get there. No need to look for me. I know what you look like." He hung up abruptly.

*Wonder how he knows that. Done his homework, I guess! But I'll finally get to see what* he *looks like, if it's really him that shows up. I'll know by the voice if he sent someone else, though.*

He arrived early and ordered a sandwich. He hadn't eaten since breakfast, and it tasted good. When he was finished, it was still well before 3. He got another coffee and settled in. But he hadn't long to wait. Whoever it was came at 2:40.

"Hello." It was the phone voice.

*Laconic in person too!*

While the phone voice ordered coffee, Hank studied him, mentally recording height, weight, complexion – everything. The man stirred in some cream and only then looked at Hank. "Gutsy, coming here. Better have something good. Tell me more about Wetzel's antics. In detail."

Hank went over everything slowly, getting no visible rise out of his listener. Then he asked: "Any questions?"

"Not about Wetzel. What do you think should be done? And what *can* be done, in your opinion?"

"This nonsense has to stop. It'll bring us down. All of us."

"How … stop him, that is?"

"I don't know. He's your guy. I figure you know him well enough to figure that out."

"Yeah, but you're the local fuzz. Tell me what we *can* do."

"I don't understand … "

"It's pretty obvious we gotta kill him. You tell me how!"

Hank's face registered his genuine unbelief. "You can't think of any other way to put the brakes to him?"

"Why? He's served his usefulness. I can always get someone else to run dope."

Hank suddenly realized just how ruthless this guy was. And he knew that he could well be treated the same way, if he weren't careful. *That FBI sting operation had better be near ready!*

"Well, I didn't sign on for that, and knowing the department down there, you best think twice about it. That could bring us down too … "

The man cut in: "Not if *you* do it. You're a clever fellow."

"I don't off people. If it's that important, get somebody else. But, like I said, you dasn't do it around Algoma. Too risky!"

"What the hell's that anyway? 'Dasn't?'"

"Dare not! It's regional."

"Didn't take you long to become Southern."

"Hey! It's been a dozen years."

"Yeah, well, regardless. You're not callin' the shots. I'll do what I want, north or south."

Hank didn't flinch or hesitate. "I'm not trying to call the shots. I'm just doin' what you hired me for: advise you of risks and help you avoid 'em. It's too risky. I'm telling you! And I should know."

The man was silent, so Hank continued: "If it'll take time to rev up whatever you decide on – and wherever, too – just know that Wetzel can get active any time. I looked for him today, but his truck was gone. I didn't call – rarely do, anyway. Usually he calls me. But the point is, he'll be back, and God knows with what surprises!"

The man pondered that. "You have a point."

"Maybe you could bring him north and take care of things here? Is there another shipment soon, or can you whomp one up?"

"Possibly. You think he'll take orders and back off? He'll know how I found out. He'll figure you told me."

"He won't dare bother *me*," Hank said. He hoped he was right.

"I'll talk to him," the man said. "But you keep me abreast of everything – and I mean everything. One more incident, and I may do him in myself." The man oozed determination.

"Just so I'm sure: You want me to watch him close, right?"

"Yeah."

"And do I talk to him, or not?"

"No need. I'll tell him he's on a short leash."

"You want me to keep real close tabs? Like minute-by-minute?"

"That sort of thing. But not literally that often."

"I should call you how often, then?"

"Whatever you think best. I want to be sure about him."

"Can't guarantee things, you know. He may be quiet one minute and not the next. You sure I shouldn't be talking with him?"

"On second thought, not a bad idea! I'll tell him to expect it. But on the cell phone, like always. And if you get the least inkling about something, I want to know – pronto."

"Got it."

"Right. Oh, before I forget," the man said and handed Hank an envelope. "Another installment. It'll save mailing. You pay the bill. I'm outta here. And I want time enough so you don't try following me."

"Wouldn't do that," Hank said, sounding professionally offended. "No biting of hands that feed me!" Hank pocketed the envelope and nodded gratefully. Always cash and, until now, always through the mail – from different suburbs, at that.

"Keep it that way," the man said and left.

Hank tried to get a make on his car, but he had parked it out of sight, and Hank never saw it leave the lot.

He took I-57 and phoned in once under way. The feds were interested to learn that Wetzel's life was in jeopardy. It might be useful future leverage, they said. Hank wasn't sure what that meant but figured he would learn soon enough. He signed off and settled in for the long drive home.

# CHAPTER XXVII

While Father John was with Googie at the truck stop the next morning, gorging on battercakes and sausage plus their "endless cups of coffee," sheriff Toler was trying in vain to reach him. Googie was enjoying center stage with Father John as his straight man, to the delight of the counter clientele. It took well over an hour, and when priest dropped tailor off, there was a surprise.

"Got your pants done."

Father John was delighted. "Thanks. I thought they couldn't possibly be ready yet."

"I lied. What's to stitching up the seat of two pair of trousers? But I didn't want to give them to you before we went. You might not pay for breakfast! They're free, by the way. No trouble! And easily worth such a nice meal."

"You're sneaky. You'll give Jews or tailors – I don't know which – a bad name!"

"Come back again when I get some cheaper wine."

"It was too long, I admit. I'll try to do better."

As Father John headed to his car, Googie shouted: "Good luck with those young fellows."

Father John grimaced, but waved pleasantly to the old man. A stop at the IGA for milk plus an impulse buy of some on-sale hamburger, and he was back at the rectory by half past 10. Breakfast with Googie was seldom a quick proposition.

The phone rang before he got to his desk.

"Sheriff Toler, Father John. Where have you been? And don't say 'on parish business'!"

"Out to breakfast with Googie Gilden – payment for fixing my pants, if you really must know. What's up?"

"Hank saw the guy from Chicago yesterday."

"He let him come up there! Good. How'd it go?"

"Well, he's a heavy dude. His man down here – well, let's just say his life's not worth a plugged nickel any more, with all the stuff he's been up to. And that complicates Hank's situation. Got time to talk over here? I'd rather not put all this out over the phone."

"Sure. Give me a few minutes?"

"Sure. Unless there's a Code Red or something, I'll be here for the foreseeable."

"Ten, fifteen minutes, then. Bye."

Father John decided to drive, since walking would take more time, and he wasn't sure how urgent this was. At the jail, he was ushered right into the man's office.

"Hi. Coffee?"

"No. Still floating from the truck stop. Thanks, though."

"Notice the new guys in the other office? FBI! It's easier to coordinate with them in this building."

"No. Didn't pay attention, I guess. Hank here too?"

"No. He's free of the desk now. I got him patrolling. It gives him an excuse to slip past Wetzel's place ever' so often. The guy up north wants him to do that, so now Hank can say he's following orders. But we want to know too. He could be plottin' something. Hank said as much yesterday to the boss man."

"You finally find out who he is?"

"Not exactly, but Hank got a good visual. Wasn't an opening to drag his name out of him. Let me tell you what went down up there. Hank didn't get a fix on the guy's car, either. But he did get one of his regular payments, and we're dusting that envelope for prints. Hank saves the envelopes that come in the mail too, but aside from postmarks, there's been nothing usable. Too many fingerprints! They kept checking, but so far, nothing. And the postmarks are from everywhere up there. Nothing useful there, either.

"The boss agrees Wetzel's dangerous, and Hank found out he's willing to sacrifice him. Even suggested Hank take care of it. But Hank nixed that and about doing it down here, too. Looks like the boss finally bought that – about it being too risky here. So Hank's to keep tabs on Wetzel. But what may go down next – or when – isn't clear to any of us. At least we know now that the Chicago guy isn't kidding around. He's willing to discard Wetzel like a used Dixie cup."

"If I understand correctly, Sheriff, everyone thinks Wetzel's a loose cannon. You just gonna wait for him to go after someone or maybe even get done in himself?"

"No. The feds are working hard at setting up a coordinated operation to get the whole drug bunch. They can walk in on most of the guys scattered around the state right now – just so's they hit them all at the same time. But they want to tie the boss in too. Hank's testimony will be a part of that, but they want something more concrete, like Wetzel and the boss with their hands on some drugs –

something like that. That operation's what we're waiting on now. Meantime, we watch Wetzel, to keep him from doing anything else."

"You said you've put better protection in place for the young men?"

"We've beefed up patrols around their homes, and I told the boys to make sure their alarm systems are active at all times. Paul had to get one, by the way. He didn't have one."

"Will all that be enough?"

"We can hope. In the past, Hank usually didn't call Wetzel, but now the drug guy wants him to. That's the only way they communicate, by the way, cell phones. Anyway, now that Hank's cleared for that, we figure he can keep warning Wetzel to lay low and also scope out if Wetzel's about to do something. That's an extra layer of protection."

"And if Wetzel does try something?"

"We'll take him in. That'll kick-start the FBI operation and, as such, isn't their first choice right now. But we'll do what we have to."

"And if you get lucky … ?"

"If Wetzel sits tight, the sting should be ready soon."

"By the way," Father John said after a moment of thought, "did Hank find out why that skeleton's so important?"

"No. All we know is that it is."

"And Hank's optimistic about keeping Wetzel quiet?"

"I don't think so. But he's doing his darndest with him."

"The young men don't know about Hank, do they?"

"No. No need. If they know him at all, he's just one of us good guys. That's enough. I've been careful not to tell them much. Can't trust them to keep a lid on things – too much of a chance something could leak out. Anyway, I don't see how knowing about Hank would reassure them any. No, they're in the dark."

"Well, I'll make sure it doesn't get out through me."

"Never doubted that, Father."

"By the way, what did Herb at the Smile have to say?"

"Sorry. I forgot to mention that. He knows how unhappy I am. It'll be a while before he tries something like that again. Imagine him thinkin' stuff like that sells papers! His circulation doesn't vary more'n ten subscriptions either way year to year – no matter what!"

Father John chuckled and bade the sheriff goodbye.

Since he was uptown anyway, he tried to think of other errands he might have there. All that came to mind was the mail, and he headed to the post office.

It was a typical pile of things: bills, junk stuff and diocesan newspapers for the back of church on the weekend. He was lazily sorting through it when Lumpy Wurtz walked across the lobby. Father John looked up at the lanky farmer, surprised.

"Hello, Richard. Haven't been out your way in a while, have I? Everything okay with you?"

"It is. I's wonderin' about you lately. Glad I bumped into you. Never seem to have time after church. Wanna come for supper soon?"

"You know I do. But it'll have to be at least a couple of weeks. Right now's kind of busy," Father John said.

"I guess so. All those things with the young fellas."

*It's like the whole town knows! Who's been spreading this? It's not all just from Hank, surely. I guess the Smile, too.*

"You mean, Pete?" Father John tried to sound matter-of-fact.

"Yeah, and all that other stuff." When Father John didn't respond, he added: "Young Eisner … "

"Oh … the piece in the Smile! Well, you know how they sensationalize."

"Maybe. But I ain't heard nobody deny it."

"The sheriff's bent out of shape, Richard. It's what he told me, at any rate."

"Hope it's just their normal exaggeratin'. Anyway, I figured you were up to your hips in work – counselin' and stuff."

"Well, I am busy, as I said, but it's a lot of things. It should slow down, as I also said, in a few weeks. If you don't hear from me by then, give me a jingle. I miss your cows!"

Richard smiled and ambled off. Over his shoulder, he said: "See you soon, I hope, Father."

The priest just shook his head. *They better get this trucker out of everyone's hair soon. Too many people in harm's way just by knowing too much, I'm afraid – and more all the time!*

He had no idea how true that was.

# CHAPTER XXVIII

Long after Father John and most of Algoma had drifted off to sleep that night, someone was still awake and roaming around outside on Ash Street. Slightly after 2 and minutes after a patrol car had passed by, flames were seen at the rear of the garage attached to 2210 Ash Street, the residence of Rick Binz. When the fire department arrived, firemen discovered someone already fighting the blaze with a garden hose. It turned out to be next-door neighbor Gilbert Wetzel, who said he smelled smoke and went outside to do what he could to protect his own property as well as his neighbor's.

The couple across the alley had called in the blaze. Tom and Tina Mitchell's bedroom is at the rear of their home, and with the privacy provided by that location, they usually cover their window with only a sheer curtain. That night they were sleeping with the window open to get a breeze and were awakened by both the sight and smell of fire. They immediately dialed 911.

Rick's master bedroom is on the opposite side of his house from the garage. Alone in the house that night, he didn't sense anything until awakened by the fire truck's siren. He explained later how fortunate he felt that his wife and child, along with the family dog, had taken their second car to visit the in-laws in Anna. He was also relieved that the damage was relatively minor. The rear wall of the garage was badly scorched and the interior had some smoke damage, but he had time to remove his car, and the fire had harmed very little inside the garage.

He thanked the Mitchells for their help and Gil Wetzel, who explained that once he started battling the flames, he had no time to call in the fire. He had thought the fire small enough that he could put it out by himself, but when he discovered it to be beyond his control, it was too risky to leave it to phone for help. So he simply kept trying to do what he could with his garden hose.

The excitement was over before 3, but the next day's report indicated that arson was suspected. So sheriff Toler soon found himself talking to the various people involved in the incident: Rick, via phone at his place of employment; the firemen who had responded; Gil Wetzel and the Mitchells. He had been leaning toward blaming youthful vandals until he talked to the last of them, Tina Mitchell, late that morning. Her husband was at work, and Tina agreed to come to the jail to tell the sheriff what she knew.

After he called for help, her husband told her that he had seen someone standing for some minutes just gazing at the fire. He was sure it was Gil Wetzel. He was also certain that the man was just standing there looking, empty-handed. Only later did he get his hose and begin to play water onto the flames that, by that time, were dancing up the garage's entire back wall.

Sheriff Toler said he wanted to hear that again from her husband, and she promised to send him over when he returned from work. Tom later corroborated the story, and thus armed, the sheriff had Gilbert Wetzel brought in for further questioning in the early evening.

On the advice of the FBI, Hank was deliberately not part of the questioning, so when Wetzel reappeared at the jail, it was only the sheriff who interrogated him. The trucker was nonplused that he should be treated as a suspect. After all, his own property had been at risk, and he had helped put out the fire. When told that he had been seen standing there watching the flames for some time, his response was that it took a few moments to assess things, and once he had done that, he went for his garden hose. When the sheriff candidly said he found that unconvincing, Wetzel started to get angry.

"Let me remind you, Mr. Wetzel, that I'll have you restrained if you don't calm down." The sheriff then informed him that under the circumstances, he wanted a lie-detector test.

At that point, Wetzel wanted a lawyer.

"Do you have one in mind?"

"No, I don't." He sounded defiant and determined.

"I think I know where to find one for you," the sheriff said.

It took Pat Kelly the better part of twenty minutes to show up at the jail, where he talked first with the sheriff.

"This is against my better judgment, Sheriff. I don't like this Wetzel. What little I know about him isn't favorable: loud, ill-tempered, standoffish! I'm only doing this as a favor, mind you."

"That, plus you know I can ask the judge to appoint you anyway. But does this mean you won't try your best?" the sheriff asked.

"No, of course it doesn't mean that. But I want to register my complaint. Okay?"

"Okay by me, Pat."

"Please bring me up to speed, then, Sheriff."

Five minutes later, he was put with the trucker, and the two spent fifteen minutes in conversation. When they indicated that they were ready, sheriff Toler joined them.

"Sheriff, the first thing you need to hear is that you cannot proceed with any lie-detector against the will of my client."

"Well, then, Mr. Kelly, I suppose we'll just have to let the judge sort out things. It's past business hours, as you know, so we'll see each other in court tomorrow morning at 9."

"I assume Mr. Wetzel will be released on his own recognizance."

"You would assume wrong, Mr. Kelly. You'll have a chance tomorrow morning to persuade the judge about the lie-detector, bail or recognizance, and whatever else. I should warn you, however, that I have a sworn statement putting your client at the scene of the suspected arson for some minutes before he reappeared with his garden hose. And the state's attorney wants to look into that."

Pat Kelly looked at Wetzel and then again at the sheriff. "I'd like more time with my client."

"You got it," the sheriff said and stepped out of the room again.

Another fifteen minutes went by before a clearly disgruntled Pat Kelly gestured to be let out of the interrogation room. "Where's the sheriff?" he asked. The guard pointed down the corridor, and the attorney went toward the sheriff's office.

"You didn't tell me about that sworn statement, Sheriff."

"When I told you there was a witness, you didn't ask what he said, Mr. Kelly," the sheriff said with the slightest hint of a smile.

"And you should know better about a lie-detector, Sheriff."

"Oh, I do, Mr. Kelly. But most folks like Wetzel don't. I had a chance there until he asked for legal help." The sheriff still had the hint of a smile.

"It's bad enough to be brought over here in the middle of supper. I thought I'd learn everything when I asked to be brought up to speed."

"Sorry. But, you know, I ain't even *seen* my own supper yet. It's too bad we're both gettin' warmed-over stuff tonight."

"Yes. Well, I'll see you in court tomorrow, then," the lawyer said in a resigned tone of voice. He turned and headed for the front door of the jail, clearly not pleased.

Most townspeople had heard about the fire by noon the day of the fire, but "suspicion of arson" didn't make the rounds until after Wetzel's court appearance the day after.

Father John reacted with sadness when he heard it, and he immediately called Rick, leaving a message on his machine. When Rick returned from work, he called Father John and told him what he had learned from the sheriff, including the arson charge. They spoke for twenty minutes, Father John careful to contain his anger but giving as much consolation as he could, even offering to have Rick sleep at the rectory that night. Rick declined, citing the obvious: with Wetzel in jail, he felt safe.

Since the sheriff hadn't called all day, Father John decided not to bother the lawman that night. The rest of his evening was devoted to finishing the prayers of the Office. He turned in rather early but tossed and turned until midnight before finally drifting off to the occasional flash of heat lightning in the western sky.

# CHAPTER XXIX

After his morning Mass when he finally had time, Father John called only to learn that the sheriff was in court and unavailable until 11 or later. It was, in fact, early afternoon before the two men were able to talk in the sheriff's office.

"I talked to Rick last night, Sheriff, and he told me about the probable arson. You have Gil Wetzel in jail for that?"

"That's what I kept him overnight for, yes. But, between you and me, lying about being away the day of the funeral is sticking in my craw too. Anyway, I think we got him for good now."

"That where it stands after this morning's hearing?"

"There'll be a trial, and he's in the pokey with us here until then."

"How soon?"

"Within the month. It depends on Pat Kelly, who's representing him. The judge is giving him time to prepare a case but doesn't want it dragging on forever. Pat thinks he'll be ready in three weeks, if not sooner."

"Will that complicate the FBI's attempts to get the drug guy?"

"A bit, maybe. I think they're going to offer Wetzel a deal. If he doesn't take it, they'll simply pick up the drug guy and all the underlings. But their case will be easier with Wetzel, so they're hoping he's agreeable to their offer."

"But they don't even know who the drug boss is."

"Hank may lure him somewhere. And they may be able to run down the phone number for him on Hank's or Wetzel's cell phone. In any case, there isn't much time. That guy's gonna miss Wetzel real soon, I figure. Maybe Hank can hold him off another few days, but not much more."

"Am I right about drug charges being federal?"

"Yeah. So's paying Hank by mail. And, if whoever killed the skeleton guy kidnapped across state lines, maybe that too."

"So Wetzel may never go to court here, right?"

"Probably. In theory, the state can pursue the arson and other local goings-on but may waive all that if Wetzel gets enough jail time on any federal counts."

"Does Pat Kelly know about the drugs?"

"Don't think he does yet, but as fast as the FBI is going to have to move, he will pretty soon. It may save him a lot of legal prepping – unless, of course, he ends up representing him in Mount Vernon or East St. Louis or whatever federal court gets the case. A'course, it could go farther north too. I really don't know for sure about that."

"So the young guys are safe now, I guess. I'm glad."

"I wouldn't absolutely guarantee that, Father. It depends on who else is on the drug guy's payroll."

"So you're not going to say anything reassuring to them yet?"

"Right. And you shouldn't either."

"Okay. But I feel for them. I'd sure like to ease their worries."

"Soon enough, Father, soon enough. And it shouldn't be much longer. Anyway, in the short term they'll be safe enough."

"You going to tell them to bring their families back home, Sheriff?"

"Nope. Not that safe yet! Better cautious now than sorry later."

"I guess I understand that," Father John said. "But I still wish I could alleviate their worries."

"The next move's up to the FBI. I think we'll be talking about what they're wantin' to do before the day is out. Hope so, anyway," the sheriff said. "Not sure, but you may have a part in that."

"Me – in a federal sting operation? I doubt it, Sheriff."

"Stay tuned," the sheriff said with a smile. He stood up suddenly, their conversation obviously at an end.

Father John rose and started for the door. It occurred to him at that moment that he had successfully maintained the secrecy of the confessional and was probably beyond further testing, now that Wetzel was securely locked away. He felt his soul swell significantly.

*Pride goeth before a fall, John. Watch it!*

# CHAPTER XXX

The sheriff emerged from the meeting with the federal prosecutor and an FBI agent, confident that everyone knew their roles in the next act. The prosecutor phoned Pat Kelly to come to the jail, and the two attorneys were closeted there for what turned out to be a heated half-hour of discussion. When they emerged at half past 11, Pat looked disgruntled but subdued.

"He understands," is all the federal attorney had to say to the others.

Pat was put into the interrogation room with Gilbert Wetzel. It took only a few minutes for the prisoner to begin speaking in loud and angry tones.

"What do you mean: 'deal?' All I did was help put the damned fire out. What's to deal? You can't get me off of that Mickey Mouse charge?"

"Drugs," his lawyer said simply.

Wetzel was not long silenced. "Drugs? What drugs?"

"Don't be coy, Gilbert. I'm your attorney. You can be open with me. In fact, you'd better be. The feds are here now, and they have you nailed, they say, on drug charges. You'll learn of that officially in a few minutes. I'm instructing you to say nothing and let them speak. Listen to what they say they have on you. And let them explain any deal they're willing to offer. Don't say a word. Once they're finished, I'll ask them to leave and we'll talk alone. Do you understand?"

"I don't do drugs!"

"That's not the charge. They say they have evidence that you've been delivering them – and for quite some time."

The color drained from Wetzel's face, and he fell fully silent, visibly shaken. Kelly could see that his confidence had eroded rapidly, like water spilling out of a child's overturned wading pool. "Just remember," he continued, "whatever they say, remain quiet. In fact, I don't want *any* reaction from you. Just listen! What they claim and what's true – or for that matter, what they claim and what they can prove – aren't necessarily the same things! We hear them out and then we talk. Got it?"

The trucker nodded, but his bravado was clearly gone.

Pat Kelly stood and motioned toward the door. A deputy had been glancing regularly through the glass in the door, and when he saw the attorney look his way, he nodded and disappeared. Within seconds, three men joined them in the room: the sheriff and two men Gilbert Wetzel didn't know.

"Mr. Wetzel. Mr. Kelly." The sheriff was gracious but business-like as he nodded to the two men. "Let me introduce Federal Prosecutor Goodman and Special Agent Wilcox of the FBI. Mr. Goodman has some things to tell you."

The man, whose identification badge hanging from his neck had "Goodman" in bold print on it, cleared his throat and began to speak softly. Pat Kelly quickly interrupted.

"Pardon me, sir, but could you speak louder? I want to be certain my client clearly hears everything the first time around."

"Certainly," the lawyer said politely and raised his voice. "Mr. Wetzel, I have here an extensive file on you." He laid a large manila folder on the table but did not open it.

"I'll be giving a copy of everything in this to your attorney shortly. But first, let me quickly apprise you of its highlights. This folder contains material that the Federal Bureau of Investigation has meticulously collected over approximately the last twenty-four months. While some of it is mundane – personal data, like your birthplace and the like – the meat of it concerns your illegal transport of drugs from a variety of locations in Southern Illinois to several destinations in Cook and Lake counties in Northern Illinois. Furthermore, the FBI knows of cash payments with regard to said drug trafficking that you have been receiving – sometimes by mail – and depositing into your personal account.

"Beyond these matters, we are aware of more recent acts you have perpetrated within this county against several young males and, in some instances, their families here in the town of Algoma, one of which acts resulted in the death of a young man.

"As your counselor will no doubt verify for you, these allegations concern a mixture of misdemeanors and felonies, convictions from which can, furthermore, result in incarceration for many, many years, if not virtually forever. There is also a mixture of federal and state crimes, which could mean more than one trial for you, should the state's attorney here choose to follow our lead.

"In short, you are facing serious charges and the possibility of heavy-duty incarceration, possibly for the rest of your natural days. Your attorney will have ample time to peruse the charges detailed in this folder." He paused to allow Special Agent Wilcox to hand a similar folder to Pat Kelly before continuing. "That folder is identical to the one I have before me. And, by the way, another folder like it is in the hands of the state's attorney of this county."

He paused to take a breath – probably deliberately, to allow the gravity of what he was saying sink firmly into Gilbert Wetzel's awareness. He continued again moments later.

"I can tell you – and Mr. Kelly can verify, should that be necessary for you – that the federal government intends to bring *some* of these charges to trial. You can be sure that your attorney will be given ample time to answer those charges, should you so desire – that is, should you desire to enter a plea of 'not guilty' and proceed to trial. But be advised that the Federal Bureau of Investigation does not pursue matters such as these lightly or bring their investigations this far without sufficient certitude as to the guilt of any persons involved.

"That is, as they say, the bad news.

"There is also good news that I am able to tell you. We are considering the possibility of a plea arrangement, the details of which we will be glad to discuss, should you, Mr. Wetzel, and your attorney so desire. We will not share the details of that plea bargain at this precise moment. We prefer that you first look at the case against you. After that, if you are curious as to what we might propose, we will gladly discuss that with you. However, be advised that such a discussion will be conducted with myself only, not with the sheriff here, or this, or any other, agent of the Federal Bureau of Investigation." He indicated sheriff Toler and Special Agent Wilcox before continuing. "We will, in the meantime, also fully apprise the local prosecutor of our intentions and the evidence upon which they are based.

"Do you understand what I have said to you? If not, you or your attorney may and should ask all the questions you like. I understand that the two of you may then wish to confer about what I've said plus the material in that folder. So – if you have questions, we'll be glad to answer them now. Otherwise, we will wait here or outside as long as you wish or need."

Gilbert Wetzel was feeling overwhelmed, as later he would come to believe that the feds wanted him to be that afternoon. He looked at Pat Kelly in a silent inquiry about what questions to ask. Kelly shook his head ever so slightly and turned to the lawmen.

"Thank you. I believe I understand the general content of what you've been saying. I *would* like time to confer with my client now and to look over the mountain of material you've just dumped here in front of us." His sarcasm was evident, but his face remained noncommittal.

The three lawmen on the other side of the table nodded wordlessly to Kelly, looked at each other and rose silently from the table. They were outside in seconds without another word.

# CHAPTER XXXI

Through the glass in the interrogation room door, Kelly and Wetzel could be seen hovering close together and paging through the massive file. The attorney was whispering earnestly to his client, who seemed desperately trying to listen, despite the dazed look on his face.

Outside that room, the sheriff wasted no time ushering the prosecutor and FBI agent to his office, where his deputy, Hank Winstrom, was seated.

"How well you know Mr. Kelly, Sheriff?" the prosecutor asked, as he settled into his chair.

"Fairly well. Why?"

"Think he'll take the deal? Or will he, at least, inquire about it?"

"I'm all but certain he'll want to know what it is. How persuasive is the stuff in your file, Mr. Goodman?"

"I'd like to think it's quite persuasive, sir."

"Well, you mentioned, for instance, that you were aware of Wetzel getting money through the mail for his drug involvement. You able to prove that?" The sheriff had obviously listened closely earlier and was not aware they had that piece tacked down.

"No, not apodictically at this time, Sheriff. But Wetzel has been paid for his part in the drug deliveries, and we're betting that it involved the mails on at least several occasions. He doesn't know what we can or can't prove on that, so it was worth throwing in. But

… we do know that Hank, here, was certainly paid that way, and, if nothing else, we can nail the boss on that."

"All I'm saying, Mr. Goodman," the sheriff explained, "is that Kelly's a good lawyer. If I can pick that out, you gotta believe he will."

"There's much more to our case than that one point, Sheriff."

"I realize that, and I'm not being critical, sir. I just don't want a few loose ends to jeopardize putting Wetzel away. His boss too!"

"I appreciate that, Sheriff. Thanks. But I think we've got a good enough case, considered *in toto*. No little thanks to you and your men, Agent Wilcox," the attorney said to the FBI man sitting beside him. The agent smiled and nodded.

"You were able to see and hear everything behind the one-way glass, Hank?" the sheriff asked his deputy.

"Yes, sir, I was."

"Anything to ask or add, then?"

"Just one thing, sir," the deputy said. He looked at the prosecutor. "Did you tell Mr. Kelly about a deal beforehand? I couldn't pick up anything in his voice or on his face that indicated surprise. Did any of you who were in there with him note any?"

The prosecutor smiled and said: "I gave the slightest little hint about that possibility when we talked before he joined Wetzel. But I certainly didn't *promise* a plea bargain, let alone share details. But, you know, you're right. He didn't show any surprise. He's cool, all right."

"Thought that might have happened – that you told him," Hank said. "But I'm also curious as to what the specifics of that deal might be, Mr. Goodman. Have you worked them out yet, and can you share them?" Hank's brow was wrinkled, as he leaned forward in his chair.

"In general, yes. In exchange for helping us get his boss, we'd let Wetzel plead to something like twenty years – as opposed to life, with or without parole. We can nab the other small fish without him if we need to, though we'll double-check our list with him, if possible, before we move on them.

"We'll also use Hank to help put the boss away. But Hank's testimony by itself may not make the case as easy as we'd like. That's where Wetzel comes in. We want to get the boss' name and location for sure from Wetzel … so as to nab him with drugs or money or both in hand. So we'll probably be bringing Wetzel along on the sting.

"Now, if Kelly's probably going to ask about the plea bargain, then my next question is: will Wetzel crumble? He looked pretty shaky just now. I'm thinking he'll want to deal, and I'm prepared to talk hard sentencing numbers in our next go-round to ensure that … if, that is, I've got him pegged right. So … what do you think? Will he cave?"

The sheriff gave Hank a glance that suggested he handle that.

"I know him better than anyone else here, and I'd guess you're right, Mr. Goodman," the deputy said. "But I hope you don't just take that for granted."

"Oh, I don't intend to. I'm experienced at this sort of thing, Deputy Winstrom."

"I'm glad," Hank said. "But let me give you something else to think about. You may find it helpful, but we'll need a few answers about it, before being able to use it. There's this skeleton, see … "

"I'm somewhat aware of that, Deputy Winstrom," the prosecutor said. "What's its full significance, do you think?"

"It's very important to Wetzel. Makes a man guess that he knows about the person's death. That could be another interesting tidbit you can use for leverage. But we got to find out more before you can throw that in your stew."

"I agree. Any ideas?"

Hank glanced at the sheriff before speaking. "Sheriff Toler is looking into missing persons around Chicago, since Wetzel came from that general area, and his boss is somewhere up there. We hope to use pertinent dental records, if we get lucky, too. We date the death to sixteen years ago, give or take. If all that falls into place, you may be able to stiffen your case against Wetzel, his boss or both."

"Has that search begun?" the attorney wanted to know.

The sheriff spoke up. "Matter of fact, it has. Nothing concrete yet, however. There are five or ten possibilities in Chicago for that time frame that they're working on. They haven't expanded the search to the suburbs yet, because the state police want to check out the Chicago leads first. I'm not sure how long all of that will take, either – they don't confide in me much, I'm sorry to report. So my suggestion's to proceed without it. You can always factor in whatever we uncover."

"Sounds reasonable," Goodman said. "We can move without it."

For the first time, Agent Wilcox spoke. “I hate to throw some cold water here, but did I understand you were listening to and viewing the conversation in the interrogation room, Deputy Winstrom?”

“That’s right.”

“Was that audio system shut off when we left? It would be a shame to have our case compromised by something like that.”

“Took care of that the moment you guys came out,” Hank said, beaming.

“Glad to hear it,” the agent said, relieved.

“There’s something else I just thought of, though,” Hank added.

“What?” Douglas Goodman said. He sounded annoyed.

“If you succeed in getting Wetzel and his boss, especially if you get them on roughly the same charges, they might end up in the same prison. State or federal – doesn’t matter. If so, I’m betting Kelly will catch that and warn Wetzel. His life might be in danger, and that could sour him on cooperating with you.”

“Good point,” the prosecutor admitted. “The good news is that they don’t have to do time in the same place. We can make sure that the judge understands we want to build that into our deal, and why … why it’s so important, that is. I’m sure we’ll get help on that.”

“So now what?” It was sheriff Toler again.

“We wait. Could be a while. Got any coffee?” the attorney asked, with confident nonchalance.

"Sure do," the sheriff said. He looked toward Hank, who was already rising from his chair.

"I can bring it," the deputy said. "But you may want some exercise … in which case, just follow me." Everyone stood and stretched before following Hank to the coffee machine in the lobby.

# CHAPTER XXXII

"Hold yourself together, Gilbert," Pat Kelly was saying to his client. "Intimidation is always one of the weapons they use on people in your situation."

"I was so sure … " Wetzel's voice trailed off.

"No time for dwelling on the past, son," the attorney said as soothingly as he could. "This fat folder here concerns us now, and it has whole bunches of things they claim they can prove. Now, I personally believe they don't have enough evidence on several items in here. Unfortunately, those things are minor issues. The big stuff they seem to have tacked down. *Seem*, I say."

"What do you mean?" Gilbert Wetzel had just jerked his head up suddenly.

"What I'm implying, Gilbert, is that they can probably make *a good bit* of the local stuff stick, and that includes at least several felonies. Arson, for the garage incident – we *might* be able to fight that one. Murder or manslaughter, however they decide to go on the Pete Hamilton death. And assault, at very least, for the two shootings – if not attempted murder on either or both of them. We may be able to dodge the shootings – I'm not sure yet. But then there's the drug charges – something else entirely, and thoroughly fraught with felony possibilities!"

"I ain't no lawyer. Make that simple for me. Can you get me off?"

"Maybe. But what I'm trying to get at is this: They've got a deal up their sleeve! Prosecutors don't do that unless they have a case they'd rather not rassle with – too complicated, too costly or too time-consuming. Or else they got some piece of a case they want badly and can't get without the help of someone like you."

"So?"

"I think they need you. Don't know for sure, but it's a good possibility. The guy told me no details as to what he might be offering when we talked before I came in here with you. But that's my best guess, they need you – probably to bring down the guy they allege you're delivering drugs to."

"I ain't involved in no drug stuff." The lack of intensity in Wetzel's voice didn't match the intent of his words.

"Gilbert! Do I have to keep reminding you that I'm your attorney? I can't represent you unless I can believe you and am absolutely sure you've told me everything. As to drug running, they sure think they've got you dead to rights!"

Gil Wetzel sat sullen and silent for a long time. Pat Kelly decided to let him stew and work through whatever bone he was chewing on. It was several minutes before Wetzel's face lit up. He bellowed: "The priest!"

"What priest? And what does any priest have to do with what we've been talking about here?" Pat Kelly was genuinely perplexed, to the point of fearing that Wetzel was beginning to lose it.

"The priest! The one in this town! He turned me in, didn't he?"

"There's no mention of a priest in this folder, Gilbert. What are you talking about?"

"Priests ain't allowed to talk." Wetzel was getting angry now.

"Gilbert, I've no idea what's gotten into you. There's nothing that I see in this mass of papers about a priest. All that's mentioned is an informer who apparently infiltrated what the feds are calling your 'gang.' And they claim to have that informer ready to testify."

"Yeah. The priest!"

"Gilbert, you're not being rational. Think about it for a moment. They identify this person as an informer *who has infiltrated your gang*. Has any priest infiltrated your operation? I don't think that's likely, but answer that: has a priest gotten inside your drug operation?"

"I'm not in a drug operation. I told you that already," Wetzel said weakly.

"And I told you to come clean with me, Gilbert."

"You don't believe me," he said, mustering a sincere look from somewhere deep inside him.

"In a word: right! I don't. I'm aware that some of the stuff in this file's also known by the sheriff. He told me things before he put me with you yesterday. You're going to have a hard time wiggling out of what he can put up against you in court. And the feds have more stuff! They know, Gilbert! They know."

"Whatever! If they claim to have anything, it's from that priest. And if he's talked about anything he says I told him, then I think you should be clever enough to make a fool of him in court, Mr. Kelly – because he ain't allowed to do that. What do they call doing that to someone like him? Discrediting a witness?" A very smug look settled onto Wetzel's face. He had his confidence and calm once again.

"You're impossible. What will it take? Do you want to confront that priest? Is that it?"

"Not particularly. You can just make a fool of him on the stand."

"He'll never get there, Gilbert. I don't intend to call him, and I can't imagine the prosecution doing so, either. He's not their informer."

The look on the accused man's face altered abruptly. "You say I can confront him?"

"You can ask to have him come to the jail to talk with you, yes. Will that convince you? We'll do it, if that's what it takes."

"It ain't a matter of convincing me. Get him over here. I want a piece of him."

"Okay – just as soon as we're finished here. First, I want to work through the possibilities of any deal they might offer and see how you want to respond."

"Deal, schmeal! I want that priest." He was shouting again.

"Okay. Okay." Pat Kelly could see that he was getting nowhere. Whatever it was in Gilbert Wetzel's craw about a priest, it was abundantly clear that it would have to be settled before the lawyer could go any further with his client. "I'll see about getting him. After that, can we then talk about the deal?"

Wetzel was silent and withdrawn. As a last measure, the attorney asked: "I suppose that it's Father Wintermann you're wanting to talk to? He's the priest here in Algoma."

"Whoever. Get me the one from Saint What's-its-name … Helena's."

Kelly reluctantly gathered up his things, rose from the table and indicated to the guard at the door that he wanted out.

He found the two feds in the lobby with their coffee and motioned for them to follow him to the sheriff's office.

Pat Kelly had enough time between interrogation room and office to work up a head of steam. "You're not going to believe this," he said, leaning across the sheriff's desk, his own face inches from the sheriff's. "He wants to see Father Wintermann."

"He getting religion?" the prosecutor asked facetiously from behind him.

"Not exactly," Pat said, straightening up to face him. "He *really* wants to talk to him, but I doubt it's about religion. I also have my doubts about putting the two of them in the same room. In fact, I'm warning you not to." Pat Kelly looked so serious that the sheriff was becoming alarmed.

"Got an arrangement here like in the prisons? You know, glass between prisoner and visitor, with maybe a telephone for them both?" The prosecutor seemed calm, in contrast to Kelly's agitation, as he made his inquiry.

"We can work something out," the sheriff said to Goodman. He then turned toward Wetzel's attorney. "Are you serious, Pat?"

"Yes, sir." Pat was clipped and emphatic.

"I can't imagine him wanting to talk to Father John in the first place – but *not in the same room?* You sure that's necessary?"

"I am. I wouldn't have put it that way, otherwise."

"What in heaven's name does he want to talk to Father John about?" the sheriff mused, and then realized that his question should have remained unasked.

"I'm not at liberty, Sheriff … "

"I know, Pat. Pay no mind. That slipped out. This is unbelievable!"

"Yes sir, but he's dead serious. And we won't get anything done until they talk, unfortunately. He's got a real case of the yips."

The sheriff saw Goodman's reaction and realized that he had absolutely no idea what Pat meant. "He's in a serious snit." The man's face remained unchanged. "He's big-time upset!"

Pat turned to the federal lawyer. "I'm sorry, but we couldn't even discuss the contents of your file, let alone the idea of a deal. You'll just have to cool your heels for a while, I'm afraid. Whatever you might have in mind, I hope you won't let my client's … eccentricities … dampen your ardor for an offer."

"I understand, Mr. Kelly. Or, at least, I'm trying to. But I warn you. If this is some cheap, stupid trick of yours or your client's, please realize that any possible offer will have a short shelf life."

"Understood," Pat said. And then, to no one in particular, he announced: "Other things await me elsewhere, some of which might actually result in revenue."

He turned on his heels and was out the door, leaving the prosecutor with a wry smile on his face. Goodman covered it by sipping the dregs of his coffee and then asking: "Any place to get a good meal around here? And maybe a bed for the night?"

“Well, it’s only a little past lunch time. We can grab a sandwich across from the courthouse. They have good soup and pie, too. And no sense ruining Father John’s lunch hour – we’ll get him here later. Maybe if we’re lucky, Mr. Kelly can achieve some breakthrough with his client that gets you gentlemen home by supper,” he said, addressing the two federal employees. “Not to mention me and Hank!

# CHAPTER XXXIII

John Wintermann ordinarily didn't take naps or even feel the need for them. But the homemade soup that a parishioner brought just after noon had tasted so good and now felt so soothing, and the air wafting through the open rectory windows was so pleasant and comforting, that he was halfway down the corridor toward his bedroom when the phone sounded. He took the call at his bedside.

He could hardly believe the sheriff when he asked him to come to the jail because Gilbert Wetzel wanted to talk.

"Are you sure he wants to talk to me, Sheriff?"

"I'm not kidding, Father. Can you come?"

"I suppose so. Have you any idea what it's about?"

"Can't say. His attorney let it be known that he desires your presence. That's all I really know. Except … "

Father John didn't like the ominous sound of that and said as much to the sheriff.

"Well, Pat Kelly suggested that you not be put in the same room with him. We can put Wetzel in the interrogation room and you behind the one-way glass. You can talk through the mike system, and if we shine a bright light on you, he should be able to see you. Least ways, I think that'll work. If it doesn't, we'll make *something* work. That okay with you?"

"I don't mind, I suppose. But will that satisfy your prisoner? And, anyway, why shouldn't we be in the same room?"

"Mr. Kelly didn't elaborate on that, but I gather that his client is more than a little worked up. Look, if you don't want to do this, Father, just say the word. I'll explain it to Pat."

"No, of course not. I'll be over. But may I ask, did you say Pat Kelly's his lawyer? How'd that come about?"

"Wetzel didn't have one and was pretty blasé about it. So I asked Pat. Wetzel hasn't complained any that I know of. Not so sure about Pat, though. I think he's unhappy about the whole thing. But he knows I can probably get the court to officially appoint him, and my guess is that's why he's staying on."

"Okay, then. Give me a few minutes. I'll be there." *Daggone it! There goes my nap. I'll get by without it, I guess.* Father John felt a sudden surge of energy. *Maybe you're too curious to feel sleepy, John!*

When the priest walked into the jail, he was quickly put with the sheriff. The first thing out of the lawman's mouth was: "It ain't gonna work, Father. The one-way glass is strictly that. Can't see through it from the other side, no matter what we do."

"So I don't talk with him after all?"

"Well, we don't have the kind of arrangement that works best for this sort of thing, which narrows our choices considerably. We need to call Pat and explain this to him. Of course, if you were to flat out refuse, that'd be the end of it, for sure. But the way Pat sounded, it's really important that you and Wetzel talk."

"Call him, then. I can wait."

The sheriff soon returned. "Pat's on his way. He didn't sound happy."

In less than five minutes, Kelly stomped through the front door of the jail.

"Now, calm down, Pat. I told you on the phone how I tried to work something out. But it can't be done. Plain as that! The only other thing, as far I can figure, is to put a guard in the room. And we could handcuff your client too."

"No, and no! No guard, no cuffs. I doubt he'd ever stand for either one. Ask him yourself, if you don't believe me."

"Well then, looks like it ain't gonna happen. Sorry." The sheriff's voice had the sound of finality to it, and Pat appeared about to react to that.

"Just a minute, please." Father John didn't like to see his two friends heating up like that. "Is there anything wrong with having a guard immediately outside the room? Gil could be told that he'd be inside in a flash if anything even started to happen. That kind of thing's okay with me."

Sheriff Toler looked at Pat Kelly, who in turn was staring at Father John.

"I don't think it's been made clear to you, Father – or maybe even you, Sheriff. Gilbert is *very* worked up. And, in his mind, it's all about you, Father. I don't know how safe you'll be with a guard outside."

"Why's he so upset, Pat?"

The attorney hesitated, looked at the sheriff, and finally blurted out: "He blames you, I think, for being here. Claims you turned him in."

The priest and the sheriff looked stunned.

The sheriff spoke first. "That's simply not true. And I think you already know that, Pat. Our inside guy's an undercover cop. Certainly not Father John. I'll admit that he and I have puzzled over some events that happened here in the county, and we talked with one another about them. But he certainly didn't *turn Wetzel in*."

Father John was about to speak, but Pat Kelly was quicker. "I am sufficiently aware of the informer, Sheriff. But I'm serious when I tell you both that, in Gilbert's mind, you're the villain here, Father John. No amount of my saying otherwise has made any difference."

"Well," the priest said slowly, "I have my own reasons for saying this, but I still believe that I can talk to him under the arrangements I just suggested. And I'd sincerely like to try. I take full responsibility for whatever happens. I'll even sign something, if either of you feels it necessary." He was one determined clergyman.

The sheriff and attorney looked at each other. Pat spoke first.

"I can tell you that Wetzel places a pretty high priority on talking with you. But I just don't know about your safety. He's not a small man, and he's decades younger than you, Father."

"I said, I take full responsibility."

"You as uneasy about this as I am, Sheriff?" the lawyer asked.

"It certainly isn't my first choice, by a long shot. You sure you want to do this, Father?"

"Yes."

"Well … " the sheriff said, looking directly at the lawyer.

"Okay." Pat said, reluctantly after a moment. "But I don't think I'll be able to live with myself if anything happens in there, Father."

"Let's do it, then," the priest said and stood up.

Father John was waiting in the interrogation room nearly ten minutes before the handcuffed prisoner arrived in the company of two guards and his lawyer.

"Father, I have explained the arrangement to Gilbert," Pat Kelly said, "and he has promised to behave. He has reiterated his strong desire to talk with you, and I've assured him of complete privacy for his discussion with you. Is there anything you want to say before we take his cuffs off and leave the two of you alone?"

"No, except that I'm surprised to see him in handcuffs."

"Standard procedure for transferring prisoners, Father," the deputy standing behind the prisoner said. It sounded very official.

"Okay, then. I'll be leaving with the guards, Gilbert. These two deputies will be right outside that door and looking through the glass the whole time. They won't hesitate to come back in here at the slightest sign of anything out of the ordinary. Do you understand?"

Wetzel nodded.

"I'll be here in the jail, just not immediately outside that door, and we'll talk when you and Father John are finished."

The handcuffs were removed and, moments later, the room held only the prisoner and the priest.

Wetzel deliberately moved his chair across the room, leaving Father John standing awkwardly beside the table in the room's center. He decided to sit at the table and wait for the other man to make the first comment. It took a few seconds.

"You broke your promise, or vow – whatever you call it. You told the police what we talked about."

Father John spoke deliberately. "So you really think I broke the seal of confession!" He paused for a breath before continuing. "I doubt you'll believe my denial but, for the record, I didn't!" His last two words were drawn out and noticeably louder than those preceding them.

"You're right about that. I don't believe you."

"How can I convince you?"

"Don't bother. When this goes to court, I'm going to expose you for a lying fraud."

"Really? I doubt that I'll be called as a witness, Gilbert, since I'm really not the cause of your ending up here in jail."

"Doesn't matter. When I expose you in court, you'll be through!"

"I'm not angry with you right now, Gilbert. I'm feeling sad that you're in this mess. And you're making things worse with this obsession of yours. It's keeping you from working out a good legal arrangement for yourself. But I guess, maybe you can't see that just now." He paused. "Will you let me attempt to enlighten you about what's really been happening?"

Wetzel didn't answer and appeared not to care about anything the priest might say or do.

Father John ignored what he thought might be an act on Wetzel's part. "Let me ask you what exactly you've been accused of?"

There was silence from the other side of the room.

"I can have the sheriff or your lawyer come in here and read out the list of things, if you won't tell me."

The prisoner stirred ever so slightly, and Father John decided to wait for an answer. Nearly a minute later, Wetzel finally said: "Drugs, and a whole bunch of stuff that's happened around town."

"And that's all?"

Wetzel didn't reply, but the look on his face said *isn't that enough?*

"What about the skeleton?"

"What about it?"

"You didn't mention it. Wasn't it on that list?"

Reluctantly, Wetzel acknowledged that he didn't think it was, but he seemed puzzled as to the significance of that.

"Don't you think it should have been? I mean, if I were telling things, don't you think that would be the first thing I'd say? I mean, murder trumps drugs any day, wouldn't you say?"

Wetzel's face slowly began to change. He looked confused but still didn't speak.

"Wouldn't they'd just love to hear about your murdering someone? I doubt there's anyone else around here, other than myself, who knows about you and the skeleton, Gilbert. And since the authorities haven't charged you with that crime, doesn't that tell you they don't know about it? Are you still so sure I've broken my ‘promise or vow,’ Gilbert?” Father John was speaking very softly and very slowly now.

The trucker began to stare at the priest. After an agonizing silence, he said slowly: “Then how do they know about the drugs?” There was a pause. “Tell me that. Who told them?” Another pause. “You did, that’s who!”

“No, Gilbert, I didn’t tell them anything – not about drugs or anything. I’ve even avoided helping those young men, who are worried silly about who has been stalking them and making their lives so fearful. I’ve gone out of my way to protect your right to the privacy of that confession, Gilbert! The police know about you from other sources. Not me!”

“Oh, yeah? Like what?”

“I’ll bet Mr. Kelly told you that someone on the inside of your operation turned you in.” Wetzel didn’t respond. “He did, didn’t he? Weren’t you listening? Or perhaps you didn’t believe him?”

Wetzel’s face was betraying him.

“I think you’d better be talking to your lawyer, Gilbert – and listening, too. I’m not the one who got you locked up, Gilbert. But I *am* someone who can help unlock what’s binding your soul so tightly. When you change your mind and decide to make a real confession, just know that I’m available. It may not sound believable, but God will forgive you in a heartbeat, Gilbert.”

He stood up but, before turning toward the door, added: “You know how to reach me. I’ll come … in a heartbeat, Gilbert.”

He smiled very gently and turned toward the door. He heard the click of the lock before he had taken a step in that direction.

# CHAPTER XXXIV

"I told you there was nothing to worry about."

"The guards said neither of you moved from your chairs the whole time," the sheriff said. "Unbelievable!"

Pat Kelly sat shaking his head.

"You ought to get in there, Pat. You should find him more tractable now." Father John was smiling enigmatically, and the other two men knew better than to ask about the cause of his Cheshire Cat face.

Pat left for the interrogation room, and the sheriff took Father John for coffee. They were cradling their hot mugs as they wandered wordlessly back to the sheriff's inner sanctum. The lawman could hardly contain himself and, as soon as the door was shut, asked: "What kind of magic did you work in there, anyway?"

"I'll take that as rhetorical, Sheriff," Father John said with a smile. "You should know that my lips are in all probability sealed. And just to remove any doubt, no comment!" He continued to smile.

"While you were in there, Pat said that if you didn't calm the guy down, he didn't think he could continue to act as his lawyer. I guess Gilbert has been one hell of a problem for him. Oops, sorry about that."

"You worry too much about things like profanity, Sheriff! Don't sweat the small stuff." Father John was still smiling.

The two men contentedly sipped their drinks. Suddenly the sheriff sat straight up in his chair. "I forgot about the feds. I best have the desk sergeant get them on their cell phones. They should be able to see Wetzel soon and, with luck, they'll be having supper at home." He set that in motion and settled back in his chair once again.

"Will it be a federal trial?"

"Looks like it. This Goodman fellow, the federal prosecutor, seems to be in charge right now, and he'll be floating a deal past Wetzel. If he accepts, I imagine that Charlie, our D.A., will be spared the trouble of trying Wetzel. See, there are guys all over the state hooked up with this drug scheme, and it's just easier to get them all in one fell swoop. However, if Wetzel doesn't go for the deal, then it's hard to say what'll happen. Might be a bunch of trials – federal, state or both. But I'm guessing it'll probably be all handled federally."

"So just drugs, then?"

"There's all that stuff around town too, including Pete Hamilton's death. But, again, it's hard to say what'll see the light of judicial day. They might not bring that stuff to court, if he takes the deal. It's just too soon to know. One way or the other, though, Wetzel's going to do time. He can make it easier on himself with that deal, but, even so, he'll end up in the pokey somewhere, and I'm anxious to see for how long. Goodman hasn't spelled out anything yet. If he follows the usual script, he'll talk tough to scare Wetzel into helping bring down Mr. Big. But what Goodman will offer for that, I'm not sure. You hankerin' for a trial here? Would you sit in if they tried Wetzel over in our courthouse?"

"No. Not my cup of tea, Sheriff. I'm just wondering right now if those young men or the Hamilton family will think that justice has been served if Wetzel only goes to jail on a plea bargain. Can they get their wishes heard beforehand, do you think?"

"Sorry to say I don't think so, especially if Goodman handles it. He doesn't impress me as sensitive at all, let alone to the wishes of people in little ol' Algoma. Could be wrong, but he seems pretty cold. No, that's not accurate. He's more interested in himself … or his career. That's the better way to say it, I think."

The sheriff read Father John's face. "Don't even think of sweet talking the guy into listening to Pete's parents or the guys Wetzel's been after. You'll be wasting your time – if he even lets you start."

Father John sighed. "Kind of suspected as much, I guess."

"You want to stick around and meet him?"

"If he's that cold, it mightn't bring out the best in me. Thanks for the coffee. I'm heading home. Tell me what shakes out, won't you?"

"You bet. Glad you came over here like that. Thanks. I must say that you got powers the rest of us are just starting to suspect!" His smile was as big as Father John's. Even a casual observer could realize that their affection for one another ran deep.

The sheriff gave the desk sergeant instructions over the intercom to inform him when the feds returned and when Pat Kelly emerged from seeing Wetzel. Then he reluctantly turned to the piles of paper before him, took a deep breath and began sifting through them.

He had only dealt with two things when his intercom buzzed. "The feds are on their way to your office," a hushed voice said. A moment later, there was a knock on his door.

"Come in." The sheriff looked up into the face of Douglas Goodman. Special Agent Howard Wilcox was close behind him. Both men were as tall as the sheriff and both heftier. "Where you been, if it's any of my business? I kind of panicked not knowing where you'd gone off to. I guess my man told you that the priest has come and gone already, and Kelly's in with his guy right now. Can't say for sure, but I'm betting they'll be ready to listen to you soon."

"Right after that nice lunch, we went driving around your fair town. Kind of quaint, actually."

Lawrence Toler wanted to wince but politely kept a straight face.

"We saw two really big churches – big for such a small town."

This time it was just too hard to suppress anything. "Surprised you missed the third one – should have been easy enough to spot in a *small town*." Goodman didn't appear to catch his irony.

"Yeah, and all those old, big homes! Must be a nice place to live." Agent Wilcox was apparently attempting to smooth ruffled feathers.

"How long's Kelly been with Wetzel?" Goodman seemed impatient.

"Not that long. He's on small-town time, you know. Thirty-five minutes at most." The sheriff believed that at any moment

Goodman would grasp his dislike at being demeaned by a self-styled sophisticate.

"Mind if I wander out to get some coffee, then?"

"I'll join you," Wilcox said. His uncomfortable demeanor told the sheriff that he wasn't as dense as Goodman, and his earlier words had the effect of softening the edge on the sheriff's voice.

"You know where it is. I'll just keep at the Mickey Mouse stuff here, if you don't mind." He indicated his desk with a small gesture and turned his attention to it before the men could even make a move for the door. He hoped they would sit outside with their coffee.

One more item from the pile was disposed of before his desk sergeant buzzed again. "Mr. Kelly's out of the interrogation room, sir."

"Thanks, Jim. Please send him and the two federal gentlemen in here."

# CHAPTER XXXV

"Have a seat," the sheriff said to the three men, rearranging several things atop his desk before giving them his full attention. "Is your client wanting to go straight to court, Mr. Kelly, or is he interested in hearing more from Mr. Goodman?"

"As I had hoped, and as I counseled him, yes, Sheriff, he's interested." Turning to the prosecutor, he said: "Mr. Wetzel would like to at least hear what you have to say, Mr. Goodman."

"Are you prepared to spell out the details?" the sheriff asked.

"I am. Want to hear about it first, Mr. Kelly? Or are you content to hear it with your client?"

"If you don't mind, would you brief me, please? If I think it in his best interest, I'll explain it to him."

"Glad to. First of all, as you know, Mr. Kelly, we have a mélange of state and federal crimes here. I talked to your district attorney … Charles … Lochner – sorry to have his name slip my mind like that. He's on board with what I'm about to say. I think he's happy not to have to prosecute and allow me to move on with the federal charges. Poor lad sounds overworked to me.

"Anyway, he'll consider everything taken care of if your client accepts the deal I'm about to offer. In a nutshell, we want him to serve somewhere between twenty and thirty years. In return for helping us nab the man to whom he has been delivering drugs for many years now, we're willing to charge him only on the drug counts – possession, transport, the like. If he accepts the plea arrangement, we'll ask the judge to use the middle of the sentencing guidelines.

We'll get him into a medium-security federal penitentiary not in the Midwest and away from the others we'll be rounding up, especially the boss of this drug ring."

"You're willing to overlook all his local crimes?" Pat Kelly sounded more efficient than surprised, like he was tacking things down before advising his client.

"That's right."

"You're not going forward with a murder or manslaughter charge over Pete Hamilton's death?" His voice now betrayed some disbelief.

"Correct."

"Mustn't trust your case against the drug boss," he said quietly.

Goodman smirked but spoke evenly. "Let's just say that we *really* don't want him to wriggle out of this – not even the least part of it – and we're thus willing to cut Wetzel a deal."

The sheriff was scowling quietly at his desk. Pat Kelly noticed.

"Sheriff, you okay with this?"

"Ain't for me to say, Mr. Kelly. But, since you asked, I don't know how the Hamilton family's going to take this. Let's just say I'm more concerned about the political ramifications than the legal. You fellows can handle that stuff. That's your bailiwick, and you ought to know all about it – more'n I do, for sure! But the Hamiltons just lost their only son, and him not married or having kids to bear their last name! Their family tree just lost a big limb. I don't think they're gonna like this."

"As you say, Sheriff, that's a political concern." Goodman was living up to the sheriff's assessment of him. "While I can sympathize, my obligation is to ensure that this nest of drug peddlers is wiped out for good. If we accomplish that, we do a whole lot of good here by preventing a huge amount of bad. And, Mr. Kelly, while I wouldn't say I distrust my case, I do want to be totally sure we nail the guy – so much so I'm willing to cut one little cog in the drug machine some slack.

"Wetzel faces the rest of his natural life in stir if we hit him with everything we've got – and you'd better believe we can prove it all, so he *will* do maximum time if all those charges are brought against him. This way, he'll get out in his sixties, unless he's stupid and acts up in the hoosegow. I'm sure you realize that, Mr. Kelly, so I'm hoping you'll make it very, very clear to him what the alternatives are."

While Goodman's face now bore a smirk that looked more triumphant than his earlier visage, the sheriff's scowl continued. "The word 'political' is indeed the right one here. Pat, you best make sure that Charlie has thought about this Hamilton wrinkle. He's running for re-election next fall, as you know. Leastways, that's my opinion. And I've probably said too much already, so I'll be shuttin' up now." The sheriff still looked less than pleased but retreated into himself and leaned back in his chair again.

Pat put the pencil in his hand against his cheek and stared at the scribbling on his legal pad. He looked up abruptly. "I believe I can advise my client as to what you're offering, Mr. Goodman. But let me ask a practical, or perhaps tactical, question. When you say you want my client to help you get his boss, what exactly will that entail? Supplying the correct name, address, etc. – or something more?"

"A bit more, Mr. Kelly. As I believe I characterized it before, we wish to conduct a sting to nab the man for whom your client has been hauling drugs. As conceived, it involves the cooperative physical presence of your client. That's why Agent Wilcox is here. I anticipated that you'd want details, and he can supply them." He turned to the man sitting quietly beside him and motioned for him to take over.

The image of an agent for the Federal Bureau of Investigation that pops into the average mind could well have the face of Howard Wilcox on it. He was a six-three, two-hundred-pound man in his late thirties or early forties, with a quiet, even serious, demeanor that made him look bright as well as capable. If you were on the wrong side of the law, you wouldn't want to go one-on-one with him, physically or in a battle of wits. He seemed the total package, and Pat Kelly sat trying to figure out what brought that conclusion so readily to mind. He finally decided it was the aura of confidence peeking from behind the man's otherwise quiet appearance. Whatever, he now gave the agent his full attention.

"What we are proposing is, on the surface, an ordinary drug delivery to the home of Mr. Wetzel's boss. Hank will ride along with your client, Mr. Kelly. For our purposes, this will guarantee that Mr. Wetzel performs as we expect and doesn't compromise our sting. But the cover story for the boss is that Hank no longer trusts your client and is along to ensure that your client doesn't bolt or in any other way jeopardize either the delivery or the entire organization. Hank will supposedly also be delivering Wetzel to the boss for final disposal.

"The truck will be accompanied by two or more cars of FBI agents, one preceding the truck on the way north and at least one trailing it. Several of those agents will be put inside the back of the delivery truck a few miles from the boss' home, to pop out when the drugs are transferred. The other agents are to remain in the cars just outside a safe perimeter and will swoop in at the last moment to secure the area and finalize the arrest.

"We'll have one or more open cell phone channels between truck and agents to allow for several things. On-going conversations can be recorded, especially those involving the boss – there will also be a recording device on Hank Winstrom. But the open channels will also serve to alert the agents in the cars to come onto the property at the correct time, and not a moment sooner.

"Gilbert and Hank will be able to identify the boss properly for purposes of legal testimony, and we'll have a search warrant as well, so we can thoroughly comb inside and outside the house and impound pertinent materials for evidence.

"We'll pull this off when a routine shipment is scheduled, but if that's not soon enough, to avoid the suspicion of Wetzel's boss, Hank will convince him that Wetzel is so high a risk to his whole operation that an earlier shipment is called for. He will insist, by the way, on transporting real drugs rather than using a phony shipment, the logic being to supposedly protect against Gilbert figuring out what's up and reacting in a way that might compromise everyone in the drug scheme.

"We'll thoroughly debrief Wetzel as to the security setup at the house so we know what to expect, and we'll impress upon him just how risky this operation can become if it goes awry. The lives of everyone involved could be in jeopardy if the sting doesn't go down as planned, and perhaps no one may be more at risk than your client, Mr. Kelly. If the operation comes unglued, the boss will recognize Deputy Winstrom and your client as turncoats. But Hank will be armed and able to defend himself. Gilbert will not. It's in his utmost interest, therefore, to tell us everything he knows about the boss, his home, the security setup and the like and to give us his complete cooperation during the sting itself.

"We think we've covered all contingencies, and we believe that this well-planned and, by that time, thoroughly rehearsed operation has a high probability of securing the arrest of the drug kingpin.

"I'll now be glad to answer any questions you might have, sir."

The entire presentation had been delivered in a soft baritone devoid of dramatic overtones, and as the agent stood quietly waiting for Pat Kelly to make the next move, the federal prosecutor gently patted him on his arm as if to say "well done."

"I think I have a clear picture of what you intend to do. Thank you, Agent Wilcox. I must say, however, that my client's cooperation is not a foregone conclusion. He is someone who operates out of a peculiar and very personal brand of logic. I'll try my best to persuade him to get onboard, but I can't promise anything."

"You do realize," Goodman said, "that this is a very good deal?"

"Oh, unquestionably."

"And that we'll put the boss on trial regardless of Gilbert's cooperation or lack of it."

"I surmised as much, yes," Pat Kelly said quietly.

"Well, then … good luck, Mr. Kelly."

"Thank you. I'm probably going to need it." He took a deep breath and gathered up his legal pad and pencils. "Sheriff, can you have Gilbert brought to the interrogation room?"

"Right away, Pat," the sheriff said, as he reached for the button to activate his intercom.

# CHAPTER XXXVI

"Hello, Gilbert. The prosecutor just explained the plea arrangement to me, and it's good – probably the best we can hope for."

"What's the bottom line?" Wetzel was surprisingly all business.

"Well, there are two parts: what they're giving and what they're asking. Which do you want?"

"Doesn't matter. Both, I guess."

"They want your help in getting your boss, and in return they'll drop all other charges except the drug stuff."

"What's that amount to?"

"Instead of probably multiple trials and certainly multiple sentences for everything they have on you – which could easily mean prison for the rest of your life – you'll be facing twenty years or so. It depends on the judge, but no more than thirty years. He has some leeway. And the feds promise a medium-security federal prison. Plus, they'll make sure you aren't in the same one as all the others they'll grab when they get your boss. Since they've promised that, I believe they'll also follow through on asking the judge to not go with the maximum allowable time. So they said just now, and I believe them."

"What's that mean about wanting my help?"

"You're to be part of a sting operation. You would make a drug delivery and they'll arrest your boss as that goes down."

"You got *any* idea how dangerous that'll be? I don't like it."

"There's some danger, of course. But measure that risk against jail forever! They'll have a lot of agents there – some even in the back of your truck. A deputy from here will be along as well."

Wetzel still didn't seem to favor the idea.

"I think you should take it, Gilbert. There are lots of little details, and I can go over them all if that will reassure you. Or, if you'd prefer, I can have the FBI do that."

"I don't know … "

"Gilbert, the incident with Pete Hamilton alone could be Murder One – and that's twenty years. Then there's the arson … "

"No need for all that. I got it. They can throw the book at me."

"Well, what's the hang-up, then? Worried about getting shot? Or do you have qualms about turning on the guy who's helped pay your bills for over a decade? What?"

No answer.

"You probably don't know it, but he's on record with their informant that you're expendable. He's willing to waste you, Gilbert. How's that for loyalty?"

Gilbert's face registered surprise. After a few seconds, he began: "Son-of-a … " The words choked in his throat. Instead, he calmly said: "Can I get a better deal if I give up something they don't know about?"

"I don't know. Like what?"

"Like where the skeleton died."

That brought Pat Kelly up short. "Let me think about that. Maybe! Just maybe!" He thought for a moment. "Are you saying that skeleton is connected to all this?"

"In a way. But, can I get a better deal?"

"You'll have to tell me more. I'm not the one offering a deal, so I can't say for sure. But more information may make things clearer."

Gilbert was hesitant.

"Look, whatever you say doesn't go past my lips if you don't want it to. But without that, I don't know how to advise you."

The prisoner sat thinking, and Pat waited.

"All right. I'll tell you a little bit, and see what you think. Okay?"

His lawyer nodded.

"I know for a fact that the man whose skeleton was found outside of town died in my boss' house."

"Why was he brought down here and buried in the woods?"

"To cover that up, of course."

"Are you telling me that the man was murdered?"

"Yes. He was."

"And in the home of your boss?"

"Yes."

Pat Kelly stared silently at the floor for some seconds, then looked up at Gilbert. "You haven't said who killed him or who brought the body here. I'm guessing those are important pieces to this tale."

"Probably. But all I want to offer them is what I've said. Is it enough to get me a better deal?"

"Gilbert, this will open a whole new can of worms. They'll want to know who killed him and why, and they won't rest 'til they uncover it all. They'll also want to know who abetted the crime by bringing the body down here. Without that, I can't possibly say whether you'll get a better deal. But my educated guess, at this point in your story, is that it stands an even chance."

Gilbert smiled, but then realized that this would ultimately bring to light his part in that drama. He had to ponder that and, as always before with complicated matters, it was a slow procedure. Pat Kelly waited.

Gilbert finally thought he saw a window of opportunity. "If I accept this deal first, does that lock it in? I mean, if I agree to help them, can they go back on their word when I then tell them this new stuff? All of it, not just what I told you so far?"

"I suppose it depends on the rest of the story, Gilbert. But, all things being equal, probably the deal would hold up."

Gilbert seemed pleased but wanted more reassurance. "What I say stays here, right? Especially if you say we shouldn't use it?"

Pat Kelly nodded again.

"Okay, then. Here's the rest of that story."

For the better part of the next twenty minutes, Gilbert Wetzel relayed what he had told Father John. He used almost the exact words of his confession, without divulging that he had confessed it to the priest. Pat Kelly sat listening intently and scribbling on his legal pad as fast as he could. When Gilbert had finished and sat silent again, Pat finished his last few jottings and looked up.

"Whew! That's some story, Gilbert."

"You don't believe me?" Gilbert asked, with a mixture of fear and incredulity.

"No, it's not that, let me reassure you. It's just that it's an overwhelming story and certainly complicates things much more." Pat's face didn't betray whether that comment meant good or bad news for his client, who was eagerly awaiting Pat's assessment.

"Let me think out loud a moment. They've shown themselves willing to overlook Pete Hamilton's death in offering you their deal. It doesn't seem too much of a stretch for them to overlook this murder, either. And from what you're saying, they can try your boss as an accomplice to it. So they'll have a conviction, which means he'll spend even more time in jail – maybe the rest of his life. That ought to please them. And it will close a cold case in Joliet. All those are in your favor, Gilbert. I'm inclined to think they'll not only want to hear it, but also that they won't let it nix the deal."

Gilbert smiled tentatively. "So, you're saying I should tell them?"

"I'm saying I think it should work, yes. But a couple of precautions before you just up and do it. Number one, I should float something by them. Number two, you don't offer this up until they formally sign off on your acceptance of their deal."

"What do you mean, 'float something by them?'" Gilbert looked worried again. "You gonna tell them everything? If so, I won't allow you. You said that stuff stays here, unless I say otherwise."

"I did say that, and I meant it. What I propose to do is to tell them in vague and very general terms that you might have more felonies to disclose and ask if they're interested. If they say they are, then I'll tell them we want a better deal."

"Okay. That's all right. Go do that. But no details – not before talking with me again! I mean it!"

Pat nodded and was tapping on the glass pane in the door within seconds.

# CHAPTER XXXVII

"Took you long enough." Goodman's face didn't show the annoyance that should have accompanied the statement. Pat Kelly figured he was kidding.

"My guy is interested, but, like all perps, he wants as good a deal as he can get. Wouldn't be easy, I told him. But he says he might have something else for you."

"Keep talking."

"He won't give it up unless you guarantee your deal."

"You doubting my word?" Goodman's face was beginning to shade over into pink.

"I'm just relaying my client's sentiments. Is it gilt-edged guaranteed?"

"You should know better than that. But, for the record, yes, it is." Goodman now looked clearly annoyed. "But as to a *better* deal, he'll have to have some very good stuff."

"Just so you know, before I go further," Pat Kelly said, "my client wants to be sure you won't back out of the deal, try to welch on it in any way or find other ways to get back at him."

"Why should I? I'm good for it – if he helps us get the big guy. Get on with it, already."

"He says he has something to add to that big guy's indictment."

"Like what?"

"Like accomplice to murder."

"I'm interested."

"He won't cough anything up until the deal is set. But assuming that he has the goods to deliver, what further can you do for him?"

Goodman thought a moment. "If it's good enough, I'll guarantee him the minimum, twenty years. No asking the judge to feel free to twiddle with something between the minimum and maximum. Twenty years! If it really blows my socks off, we'll dicker."

Pat Kelly realized that there would be no dickering. Goodman would never let Wetzel get off with less than twenty years. And he would never, therefore, admit that anything Gilbert had to say was off-the-chart valuable. This was as good as it would get. "Twenty years, then. I'll put it to my client. Of course, if he gets lucky with what he has to say, all the better! See you in a few minutes."

Gilbert seemed pleased at what Pat Kelly explained to him. "So what now?"

"We'll bring the prosecutor in here and have him formally offer you the deal. Nothing will be signed, but we'll have a witness or two along, so you can trust that they won't back off later. Once you formally accept the plea bargain, you can then tell him what you told me. But dribble the information out. Make him come get the whole story. I'll be here to advise you, and you can always ask me how to proceed or how to phrase something."

"And if he gets the whole story, are you sure I won't go down for murder, too?"

"As I said before, if they're willing to let a local death slip by, I can't imagine them being that concerned about one up north sixteen years ago. It should be enough to get your boss for it. Anyway, I put it to him lots of different ways, and he kept saying that it's a solid deal, no backtracking or anything else for you to worry about."

"Okay, then."

"Oh, before we get them in here, there's a little more. Before giving your new information, they'll want your boss' name, address, etc., and you should answer any questions they may have about him. And, if I were you, I'd also have them completely explain the details of the sting – all that, before you say anything new. Got it?"

"Think so."

"I'll go get them, then. But know that you're liable to find out who their informer is. If not, and you still want to know anyway, feel free to ask. The sooner you know, the better, in my opinion."

Wetzel looked perplexed, but he nodded, and Pat Kelly stepped to the door to be let out.

Soon, Pat stepped back into the room and was followed by several others. More chairs were brought in, and after everyone was seated around the interrogation room table in the center of the room, Douglas Goodman reintroduced himself to Gilbert Wetzel, this time using his first name as well as his last. He had his game face on and spoke very slowly and deliberately. The sheriff accompanied him and brought another deputy along. Agent Wilcox also was present.

"Mr. Wetzel, I understand you are interested in accepting the plea arrangement I mentioned to your attorney."

"Yes, sir."

"Just to be sure you understand, let me go over the offer. In exchange for your assisting in our sting operation to bring down the man to and for whom you have been delivering drugs these past fifteen-plus years, we are dropping all other charges and offering you between twenty and thirty years in a medium-security federal penitentiary on the drug-related charges. The exact sentence will be left to the judge's discretion, although we will strongly suggest that he lean away from the maximum suggested by the sentencing guidelines. We will also ensure that you do not end up in the same federal facility as any of the others involved in this drug ring. Is that what you were told by your lawyer?"

"Yes, it is."

"Well, then, do you accept our offer?"

Pat Kelly put a hand on Gilbert's arm and whispered something to him.

"Sir, would you explain the details of how you're going to arrest my boss before I say yes or no?"

"Gladly. Agent Wilcox?"

It took the agent ten minutes to completely recount all the details. After his presentation and the answering of several questions, Gilbert indicated that he was ready to accept the federal deal. Then Pat Kelly whispered something else to him, and Gilbert asked: "But first, will you tell me who your informant is?"

Douglas Goodman was momentarily startled. He looked at Pat Kelly and then at sheriff Toler, before stammering: "Are you sure you want that information now?"

He addressed the question to Pat Kelly, but Gilbert answered it. "Yes. Won't that come out anyway? Better now."

The prosecutor nodded, looked once again at the sheriff and spoke. "I'll be glad to divulge that … unless you would rather, Sheriff."

Sheriff Toler gestured in deference to the prosecutor, who then said simply: "Deputy Hank Winstrom."

As Pat Kelly had suspected, this appeared to disturb his client. He quickly leaned over to whisper: "Careful, now. No outbursts. Stop to think. It doesn't really matter who gave the information, does it?"

This appeared to calm Wetzel. He pulled away from his lawyer to look the prosecutor directly in the eye. "Thank you," he said, with surprising evenness.

"I suppose it is better that you know now," the prosecutor said, "because he is the deputy Agent Wilcox said would be riding north with you when we spring our trap. You see, it will be perfectly acceptable to your boss that he accompany you, since he's not only known to him, but he's the one to whom the boss said you couldn't be trusted any more. It serves our purposes wonderfully well on all counts, I'm sure you can agree."

Gilbert didn't speak, and Pat feared that he might be building toward an outburst. He kept watching for telltale signs, but none were appearing thus far. He would probably have to deal with this later, he knew.

After activating a small recording device, Goodman asked: "Mr. Wetzel, are you ready to accept our offer."

He glanced at his attorney before saying: "Yes. I accept it."

Pat Kelly immediately spoke. "Sheriff Toler and Agent Wilcox, do you join me in attesting to the facts of the plea bargain, as well as the acknowledgment and acceptance of them by my client?"

Both men nodded, but at Pat Kelly's urging, then said aloud that they did so attest. The tape recorder kept whirring.

"Then, let me ask Agent Wilcox to take down pertinent information from you, Mr. Wetzel. Just speak out your answers slowly and distinctly for the tape machine and for him to copy down on paper, please. Let's begin with the name of the man to whom you have been delivering drugs these past fifteen or sixteen years."

"Clayton Drexel."

It was the first time any of them, including Hank Winstrom behind the one-way glass, had heard his name. It took the agent another few minutes to get the rest of the information, and when he had finished, Douglas Goodman directed him to leave the room. "He's getting that information off to FBI headquarters," Goodman explained.

"Now, I believe you may have something further to tell us, Mr. Wetzel – is that correct?"

Pat Kelly spoke before his client could answer. "Would you please state the terms of the plea bargain for the record, Mr. Goodman. And then, would you please turn that tape machine off?"

"Of course," the prosecutor said, with the hint of a smile playing across his lips. It had been worth a try, he thought.

When the machine was clicked off, Gilbert spoke. "I know where the man whose skeleton you found died."

"Really? Where?" Goodman did not act impressed.

"In Clayton Drexel's home."

That got his attention, and the sheriff's as well.

"But why, then, did he end up buried in some woods down here, Mr. Wetzel?" Goodman asked the question superciliously, in an effort to gain back some momentum.

Wetzel didn't allow that to happen, even though he seemed unaware of the little game the prosecutor was trying to play. "To cover up the circumstances surrounding his death, of course." Gilbert had taken to his coaching and was performing quite well, in his lawyer's opinion.

"Are you saying there was foul play involved?"

"Yes, sir. His throat was cut."

Goodman, without thinking, reached for the tape machine, and Pat Kelly instantly wagged his finger at him.

His hand stopped in midair, but he continued to grill the prisoner: "How do you know that, Mr. Wetzel?"

"Because I was there."

Pat Kelly spoke up. "Is this the kind of thing that merits an amendment to your offer, Mr. Goodman?"

"I'd have to say that it does, Mr. Kelly. Yes, I would."

"Then before Gilbert goes any further, are you prepared to make a firm offer to him?"

"Well, I think you'd have to agree that I'm within reason in wanting to hear more details, wouldn't you, Mr. Kelly?" Suddenly everything was very formal.

"And I think you could agree, could you not, Mr. Goodman, that my client doesn't have to continue with this, were he to so choose? In other words, Mr. Goodman, do we have your word that you will at very least offer him a guaranteed minimum sentence of twenty years?"

"You know, I can pursue this on my own, Mr. Kelly."

*Don't threaten me, turkey!* "Not without a whole lot of time, effort and money – especially money. And without the cooperation of my client, I might add. Identifying the victim alone may take years!"

Goodman contemplated that for a moment, and then softened. "It *is* in our best interests to expedite the solution of this case. You have a point, Mr. Kelly. I'll promise what you ask."

Pat turned to the two local lawmen. "And should it become necessary, you both will be willing to swear to hearing that promise, won't you?"

"Yes," they said together.

"Then, Gilbert, would you mind telling Mr. Goodman the whole story?" Pat sat back, relieved.

Wetzel's rendition was remarkable. For this third telling of his story, he chose virtually the same words he had used earlier. He seemed to have memorized it, but it was his remarkably uncreative personality that was driving his performance. It was effective, nonetheless, and eventually Douglas Goodman stopped him.

"I want to get this recorded, if you don't mind. And then, once it can be transcribed, I'd like your client to sign it. Is that all right with you, Mr. Kelly?"

"Fine by me."

"And, by the way, very clever of you, Mr. Kelly. We get the accomplice to the murder, and the murderer gets off. Very clever."

"We can talk about that later, Mr. Goodman. In the meantime, Gilbert, would you mind starting over, once that tape recorder is turned on?"

# CHAPTER XXXVIII

It had been a long day, all three men agreed, and not one of them was unhappy to see it end. They sat sipping coffee with the sheriff and enjoying the afterglow. Douglas Goodman was the first to speak.

"I have to hand it to you, Mr. Kelly. Getting me to promise before finding out your guy was in on the murder. Very clever! Caught me off-guard. I do know better that that. Timing's everything, I guess."

"Thank you. It *is* all in the timing. That, and you got a little greedy, I think. Thanks, too, for your promises to my client, by the way. And to think you felt I might not represent him fully, Sheriff!"

"I merely asked a question, Patrick." Lawrence Toler was smiling.

"Don't take it so hard, Mr. Prosecutor. You're still getting someone for that murder. And you, Sheriff, can now close that cold case for them in Joliet."

"Yes, and the knives we got from Wetzel's place not only confirm that he slashed those tires, but now we also know he used one of them on that poor teacher. What did Gil say his name was?"

"Weatherby. Jay Weatherby," Pat said to his local lawman.

"Wanna see 'em? They're impressive in a scary kind of way."

"Maybe tomorrow. Right now, I'm too bushed for anything but savoring this coffee, Sheriff." The prosecutor seemed content.

"Won't the Smile have a field day with this one," Pat said.

"The Smile?"

The sheriff eyed Pat as he elaborated for their guest. "Our weekly paper, Mr. Goodman. Not known for aggressive reporting, but strong on creativity, if you get my drift."

The sheriff, Pat realized, was still smarting from the recent "rumor" article. "I imagine you'll help them stay on the straight and narrow with this story, Sheriff."

"If I thought it would teach Herb anything, I'd write the damn story myself." He chuckled.

The federal prosecutor shifted in his chair. "I'm hoping we can finish this off soon. Your deputy's been trying to reach our target, hasn't he? Hope Mr. Drexel doesn't get elusive on us just when we're ready to pounce."

"Hank'll be in here after he gets him and sets up a delivery."

"Can you trust Wetzel to drive all the way up to Homewood without causing trouble or derailing our plans?"

Pat Kelly spoke up. "He knows you're his one hope of seeing the real world again before he dies. He'll be a pussycat. But I'm wondering, will Winstrom be armed accompanying him in that truck?"

"Sure. Why not? It won't be worn as a sidearm, but he'll be packing. He's the first line of defense, in case the agents in the cars are tardy or whatever. When will you be practicing the drill with your team, Mr. Goodman? Hank expects to be a part of that – I expect that, too." The sheriff could be forceful when he wanted to be.

"Oh, he will be, for sure. First thing tomorrow morning, we'll do the drill. Several times, to be absolutely sure. Standard procedure, especially when we have someone new, like Winstrom."

"You'll find him a quick learner. Perhaps you didn't know, but he did your academy some years back and got top marks."

There was a knock on the door. "C'm in," the sheriff said.

Hank Winstrom popped his head inside.

"Speak of the devil," the sheriff said and flashed an impish smile.

"Can't stay. Supper's getting cold, my wife phoned to say. Just wanted you to know that we're good to go the day after tomorrow. Should allow time to coordinate the arrests of everyone else, Mr. Goodman. What time is your practice?"

"Tomorrow morning at 9. We're meeting here at the jail."

"Thanks. See you then. Nice show today, by the way. Glad I got to watch." He closed the door quickly.

"That man's on a mission. If he's as hungry as I am, I can understand it." The sheriff rose from behind his desk.

"I can take a hint," Pat Kelly said and stood up as well.

"Just when I was beginning to feel comfy!" Douglas Goodman said, slowly rising from his chair. "I'll see you tomorrow, then, Sheriff. But I may not see you again, Mr. Kelly – nice doing business with you!" He extended his right hand, and Pat shook it politely.

"Don't you forget about the deals we've struck, Mr. Goodman."

His attempt at light-hearted humor did not bring a smile to the prosecutor's face. Instead, he said: "You just make sure your man is the soul of cooperation the day after tomorrow when we go after

Clayton Drexel." His last two words sounded sarcastic, as though he either despised the man or was making fun of his name. Or both.

"Don't you worry none! You scared him enough. He'll do the job."

"Shoo," the sheriff said. "I told you I was hungry. Tomorrow, Mr. Goodman – and soon enough with you, I imagine, Mr. Kelly." He was smiling but determined as he waved the two men out of his office ahead of him.

# CHAPTER XXXIX

"I'll be glad to," the sheriff said to the deputy. He picked up the phone and called St. Helena's. "Not too early for you, I hope."

"No. Just got back from church, Sheriff. What can I do for you?"

"Gil Wetzel says he wants to see you."

"Again? I thought I satisfied everything yesterday."

"You probably did. This time, I'm told, he's not as ornery."

"I suppose he didn't say what he wanted."

"You would be right about that. I certainly haven't the foggiest what this is all about, and I suspect my deputy wasn't told either. All I know is, he'd like to see you. Can you come?"

"Sure. Any rush?"

"Don't think so. Why?"

"I've got someone here who was at church just now. She wants a Mass or two for her relatives. Do I have fifteen minutes?"

"Sure. Take your time. I'll see you when you get here. Better still, just tell the desk sergeant, and he'll put you with the prisoner."

"Okay. Oh, before you get away – are they wrapping things up tomorrow?"

"That's the plan, yes."

"Dangerous?"

"Oh, there's always an outside chance of that, but this is pretty well-organized. Should work out okay."

"Hope so. I'll be there shortly." Father John put the phone down and turned to his parishioner. "This shouldn't take long, Flora.

When would you like those Masses? I've got the schedule book right here."

When he arrived at the jail, it took but a few seconds to put him in the interrogation room. Ten minutes later, Gilbert Wetzel was led in. Father John stood to greet him. "You wanted to see me, Gilbert? Are you still upset with me?" The guard uncuffed Wetzel and withdrew.

"No. It's not that. I have some other things to tell you," Gilbert said after the lock sounded behind the guard.

He seemed surprisingly calm – not exactly serene, but more composed than Father John had ever seen him. It was intriguing, a minor mystery of sorts to the priest.

"I'm glad you came. I want to tell you that what I said at the rectory about that teacher wasn't entirely true."

Father John almost asked if that meant the man had not molested his brother but held his tongue.

"I have prayed for him every once in a while."

"Does that mean you have forgiven him?"

"I don't know. But a year after I killed him, I got to thinking that he maybe couldn't help himself or something. I realized it wasn't as black and white as I'd made it. I don't know. It was confusing. Anyway, I started praying for him every so often. Maybe, like you said, he didn't deserve to die for that awful thing. Is that forgiveness?"

"Sounds close. But why's it important to tell me that now?"

"Because maybe I *am* sorry I did that."

"Would you like absolution, Gilbert?"

"Well, I'd like to talk about it, anyway. What's that mean, forgiveness?"

"That God and the Church forgive you all the sins you confess."

"Yeah, but what I mean is, is it that simple? I just say I'm sorry?"

"It includes your firm intention not to sin that way again. But don't take that too literally, Gilbert. I know you most likely won't have the chance to murder again or even be tempted to. It goes beyond that … to your *intentions*. Those must change. Asking for forgiveness means you'll seriously try to change how you think about and treat other people."

Gilbert looked puzzled.

"I can put it more simply, Gilbert. Instead of thinking mostly about yourself, start putting others first. That's really what we mean by 'love,' Gilbert. Asking to be forgiven is really saying you'll try very hard to put love more firmly into the way you live. Are you ready to do that? If you are, I not only can, but will, offer you absolution … in a heartbeat, Gilbert." Father John had begun speaking softer and softer, until his last words were almost a whisper.

The prisoner startled him by breaking into tears. "I want to try."

He supposed that he was breaking the rules, but Father John got up, went 'round to Gilbert's side of the table, lifted him from his chair and held him. Now he was crying full force, and Father John was even more surprised than the guard at the door, who was by then frantically fiddling with the lock. By the time the door was open,

Father John was silently mouthing to him: "It's all right. You can leave us alone."

The guard hesitated, and his concerned look didn't fade. Father John gently jerked his head, in effect telling him to leave, and the guard reluctantly retreated from the room. Father John continued to wordlessly hold Gilbert Wetzel, and when he next glanced at the door, he saw the sheriff's face. Father John just lifted his eyebrows ever so slightly, and the lawman nodded and disappeared. It was a full two minutes longer before Gilbert showed signs of regaining his composure.

Father John guided him to his chair and then went to his side of the table. He leaned across the table and talked softly. "Do you want time to yourself, or are you ready to make a confession now, Gilbert?"

"I'd like to talk for a while, if you don't mind, Father."

The priest nodded.

"I've had time to think, especially the past day or so. I never thought very far ahead before. I just took things as they came. Oh, I'd be ready for whatever any job called for, but as to other things, they were usually spur-of-the-moment. The only thing that didn't work like that was every so often when I thought about that teacher. Did you ever learn his name?"

He hadn't, and Father John shook his head again.

"His first name was Jay. I'd think of him every so often, as I said. At the strangest times … just out of nowhere it might happen! And then I'd say a prayer. But I never thought more about it because I think I was too scared to. Didn't know where it might lead to.

Anyhow, I never thought out other stuff either … just took things as they came.

"But now I've been thinking a lot. I've come to believe that I was afraid to challenge my boss. His name's Clayton, by the way. And, anyway, the money was so good! But you know, I never spent it on anything special or anyone special, either, even when I still had my parents. There were just us two boys, and my folks died a few years ago. So even the money wasn't important, I now realize. I just put it in the bank ... for I don't know what. It's kind of silly, really. Isn't it?"

He didn't wait for an answer, and Father John didn't attempt one.

"So I keep asking myself, this past day or two, why I did all that. I could've stopped. I'd have to move away, but I had all that money. It's not millions, of course, but it's way more than I'd need to start over somewhere. But I never did. Didn't think it through, 'til now. Wish I had!

"And I've been thinking of the people I hurt, too. Not just the men here in town, but all the people who took the drugs I kept bringing to Clayton. Has to be thousands by now … " His voice had trailed off, and he finally fell silent, staring at the table.

Father John began tentatively: "I remember raising a question about what good all the stuff was that you were doing around town, like the shootings." He stopped before he finished his thought, not sure if he was approaching things in the best way.

Gilbert looked up. "Yeah, I remember that. Didn't pay it any mind at the time, but I have since yesterday. Kind of stupid – like even killing Jay in the first place. I could've scared hell out of him and left it at that. I could have turned him in, but I remember at the time thinking that it might be hard to prove with my brother gone and all. But there were other things I could have done and didn't. Most any of them would be better than this now.

He stared at the priest. "But that ain't why I'm sorry now. I ain't sorry for myself – I'm sorry about what I did. I think I'd like to change because I don't like feeling this way. I know I brought it on myself, and I'm glad to know that I can change it. Though, other than saying I'm sorry, I don't know what else to do about it. I'm hoping you do!"

Father John was touched. "You've just eloquently expressed your sorrow in a big way, Gilbert. The easiest thing I can do now is to offer you absolution. But you've raised another question: How do you go about living differently? That will take more discussion, I do believe. What about absolution first?"

"What do I do?"

It was over in several more minutes, and the look on Gilbert's face told Father John that something impressive had happened to the man's spirit. *Deo gratias!*

"You want to live differently – is that what I'm hearing, Gilbert?"

"Yes, but how? I'm going to prison. I doubt if there's much room for love there."

"You might be surprised. There are lots of ways you can help others in prison: acts of kindness, curbing your temper, helping someone learn to read, or sharing your skills with others. I hear you know a lot about engines. Maybe there's a shop in the prison you'll end up in. If so, you could teach engine repair."

"I wish there was something I could do with all that money in my bank."

"There may be," Father John said, brightening. "Talk to Mr. Kelly. I don't know the legalities of that sort of thing, and I suspect you won't have access to much, if any, of that money while you're behind bars. But he'd know. And he'd also know how to legally make it available so it can help people."

"You don't know any place like that, Father?"

"I can suggest some charities, Gilbert, but I don't know all the legal ins and outs about pulling off helping them right now. That's where Mr. Kelly comes in. He's got all that at his fingertips."

"Well, like what kind of charities? Maybe we can figure that out without Mr. Kelly, and all he'll have to do is push a button or two."

"It's much more important that any gift of yours make sense to you, Gilbert. I'd just be reciting names of charities … "

"I think I understand," he cut in. "I'd like to help people like that teacher … and like my brother."

"Really excellent, Gilbert! And Mr. Kelly can help you do that, I'm sure. Want me to get hold of him so that when he sees you next, he'll be able to settle it in probably one meeting with you?"

"Yeah, I do. But, Father, tomorrow I go with them to arrest my boss. I don't know if … "

Father John realized for the first time that Gilbert was afraid of what might happen up north, that he might not be alive tomorrow evening. “Do you want me to have him come as soon as he can today?”

“Yes. I’d like that.”

“I’ll get him right away, Gilbert.” He rose and heard the guard putting his key into the door. “But before I go, I have two things to tell you. I’m proud of you! And I’ll be back to pray with you any time you ask after tomorrow, Gilbert. I’ll be back in a heartbeat!”

His conversation with Pat Kelly took only a few minutes. And once the lawyer arrived at the jail, he spent only fifteen minutes with Gilbert. The priest shared a meal that evening at the lawyer’s home, where they agreed that God’s grace was interesting, to say the least. It triumphed over the bumbling of priests, the reluctance of lawyers and even the mysteries of a murderous heart.

# CHAPTER XL

The team was gathered at the jail by half past 8. Someone had already brought Gil Wetzel's truck, and the FBI office inside the jail was humming. Calls were coordinating the many arrests planned for that afternoon around the state. Just before 9, all the local teams were in synch with the main operation that Agent Wilcox was heading. The agents around the state confirmed that they were not to move on anyone until the trap was sprung at Drexel's place in Homewood, at which time Wilcox would give the go-ahead.

Hank Winstrom was scanning an Illinois road map and carefully rechecking the route to the home of Clayton Drexel. It wasn't quite time to bring Gil Wetzel from his cell, where he sat in civilian clothes, waiting patiently for a guard to spring him. Sheriff Toler had appeared promptly at 8:45 along with Douglas Goodman to act as the apparent official send-off party.

"Hank, let's check the cell phone you'll use to stay in touch with Wilcox. I want to be sure the conference link works to our phone here at the jail." Sheriff Toler seemed in high spirits. After the two were satisfied that the technology was at peak performance, the sheriff turned his attention to a deputy just coming from inside the jail.

"Sure. Bring Wetzel out. No worry about him out here – he won't be going anywhere. Bring him here to me. And no need for cuffs."

Douglas Goodman was busy glad-handing all twelve of the FBI men who would accompany Wetzel's truck in three cars. With

Hank and Wilcox, that made fourteen men who were to bring down the drug kingpin, as they had taken to calling Drexel. One car would lead the convoy, and the other two would trail Wetzel's truck. With Hank riding shotgun in the truck, the lawmen felt that nothing could go wrong on the way up. Later, they would accompany the truck back to Algoma after Drexel's arrest and incarceration up north. Plans to jail the others arrested that day in various local facilities were already in place. Wetzel would then be kept at Algoma before removal out of state, it was hoped, by week's end.

The sheriff, prosecutor and special agent conferred one last time. It was the consensus of the triumvirate that all was in place, and the four vehicles got on the road at two minutes after 9. Everyone in the party, including Wetzel, had enjoyed a hearty breakfast earlier – many of them at the truck stop – because once under way, there were to be no interruptions before the midafternoon arrest. The auspices were great, morale high, and everyone had victory within sight.

After they left, the sheriff turned his immediate attention to his desk, and by noon had made such headway that he decided to reward himself with a light lunch. He would have plenty of time before 2, at which time he planned to hunker down and monitor events up north on a minute-to-minutes basis.

So he called Father John at 11:45. "Let's get lunch."

"I can do that. Any word yet?"

"Just the hourly reassurance calls from around the network. So far, so good!"

"See you at the deli by the courthouse square in a few minutes, then." Father John suddenly felt hungry.

# CHAPTER XLI

As they waited for chef salad and iced tea, Father John asked if the sheriff had talked to Pat Kelly that day.

"No. Why?"

"He saw Gil yesterday after I was in with him."

"Hadn't realized."

"Yes. And he and I had supper last night."

"So … ?"

"He's going to be able to help Wetzel spend the money he's been saving all these years. I was surprised to learn he lived pretty simply."

"Really? But are you sure about Pat being able to spend his money? I thought the feds were impounding his financial assets."

"Seems they can't keep it all. For some strange reason, Wetzel kept his regular income separate from what he was paid by the drug guy – Drexel, right?"

"Yeah. Clayton Drexel. What a name! He wouldn't make it around here long with that moniker."

"Well, keeping it separate like that, Kelly says, makes it easy to identify what was legal and what was drug-related. By the way – he never spent any of the drug money, if you can believe that! That drug money's theirs, all right, and any fines from the court would come from the other monies. But Pat seems to think there won't be any fines, so the rest of his dough can go for what Wetzel told Pat about yesterday. It's all signed and legally taken care of."

"Any surprises? You act like there are."

"I think so. He'll keep some money against the day he gets out of the slammer, of course, but Wetzel wants a lot of it to go for therapy for sexual abuse perpetrators and for their victims."

"You don't say! That *is* a surprise. Where'd that come from, I wonder?" The sheriff flashed a sly grin.

"Don't go laying that on my doorstep, Mr. Know-it-all. It was all Wetzel's doing. Pat and I were as got by that as you are, I imagine. Pat says it'll take time, though. The feds and the court are going to haggle awhile until it all shakes out. But he's sure quite a bit of money will be available eventually."

"You can act innocent all you like, Father. I know better. He wouldn't have done that all by himself. You continue to amaze me."

"You're welcome to your opinion, Sheriff, and if you insist on believing the unbelievable, I won't contradict you – as long as you keep paying for meals!"

"I get the hint. I'll grab today's check. But don't get attached to the idea of free lunches, no matter how highly I might value your clerical skills." The smiles came easily to both their faces, just as the waitress arrived with drinks and the promise of salads soon. The sheriff sat shaking his head in a mixture of admiration and disbelief.

Back at the jail, he awaited the 2 o'clock phone-around and realized that he was getting edgy. When it came, the voice of Agent Wilcox indicated that the next transmission would occur when the convoy was stopped several miles from Drexel's address, where they would put into effect the final stage of their plans. He estimated that to take forty-five minutes. Radio silence was to be in place again until then, barring an emergency anywhere on the network.

The sheriff tried to turn to his paperwork backlog, but found himself too nervous. He went for coffee, looked in on several offices, only to find things routine, and eventually found himself back at his desk with twenty-five minutes to kill.

The phone line crackled to life fifteen minutes earlier than planned, however. The voice of Agent Wilcox alerted everyone to the remaining details of the sting. "Deputy Winstrom's cell phone will be left on with his volume on high so we can hear the drug transfer. *Absolutely no one* is to violate radio silence until you hear my voice," he said, imperiously.

"And once again, just to be sure we're all on the same page, let me review what happens then. Aside from the three agents who are in the back of the truck, the others will immediately proceed to Drexel's house. The SWAT agents surrounding the address should all have a clear line of fire on Drexel's place. I'd like to hear about that from them now." Each unit checked in: three electrical linemen out front, two telephone linemen at the rear of the house, a mail carrier on the sidewalk out front, and three agents at upper windows of each house beside Drexel's, plus one across the street. All said they possessed a clear line of sight.

"Fine. Now here's the final drill. Winstrom and Wetzel will lure Drexel from the front door to the rear of the truck. Drexel's under the impression that as soon as Wetzel hands him the drugs, Winstrom's gun will be out with the intention of hustling Gilbert into the house. He'll turn it on Drexel instead and, as the agents inside the truck storm out, we should have Drexel on the ground as the mobile units arrive. There is to be no firing of weapons – I repeat, no firing of weapons – *unless* Winstrom or I authorize it *or* one or more SWAT units get a visual on any armed resistance. We've been led to expect nothing like that, but the SWAT guys are our guarantee against that kind of surprise. We're hoping for a swift and quiet resolution to this. Any questions?"

There was a full fifteen seconds of silence before he concluded: "You have your orders. We're a minute from success." The silence that followed was maddening for sheriff Toler.

The next thing he heard a half-minute later was Hank Winstrom talking quietly to Gilbert Wetzel as they pulled into the driveway in front of the house. Then he heard the front doors of the truck opening and slamming shut, the crunch of footsteps on gravel and the distant sound of a doorbell from within the house.

The dialogue at the door was brief, and more gravelly footsteps followed. Just after the actual transfer, the rear doors of the truck burst open, and a scuffle ensued with a lot of noise. Suddenly there was a shot and then two more shots and a lot of shouting.

The sheriff made out several things amidst the noise.

"He's hit."

"The front window … the window ... "

More shooting! It was hard to count the number of firings or tell whether they came from close at hand or some distance, but it was more than two or three. Glass had broken, and the shouting had continued unabated for some further seconds. Later, sheriff Toler was unable to say how long it had lasted, but Agent Wilcox told him that the FBI replay of the fracas clocked in at less than thirty seconds.

He sat at his desk, unwilling to clog the audio network and agonizing over the possibilities, too many of which didn't seem good. Special Agent Wilcox had been barking orders for several minutes before he called the sheriff's name.

"I'm here, Agent Wilcox."

"Sheriff, we have good news and bad. Drexel's in custody and unhurt, and a lone bodyguard's dead inside the house after discharging his weapon four times. We think Hank took him down, but he suffered multiple hits, so at least one of the SWAT guys is to be thanked, too.

"No agents suffered injuries, but Hank was grazed at close range by the bad guy at the window, and Gil Wetzel is on his way to a hospital with several wounds to the arm and chest. His condition is unknown at this time. We have begun combing through Drexel's home as we speak, and the local PD – on alert for the past hour – is cordoning off the scene now. All in all, a resounding success, despite one minor and perhaps one major casualty on our side!"

"Thank you, Agent Wilcox. Glad to hear you have the bad guy. Have Hank contact me on his off-network phone when he can."

"Will do. We've got some mopping up to do. If the medics give a go-ahead, I'll have your deputy brought back by some of our men. The truck stays here 'til we learn where they want to try this case. It now bears a few bullet holes, which will surely become part of the case. I'll have Hank get to you, but I'm estimating a few minutes yet for that. Headquarters tells me we have all the minor bad guys in custody, too. Oh, and I'll get a report on Wetzel as soon as I can."

"Ten-four," an emotionally drained sheriff said as he slumped back into his chair. "Poor Wetzel," he said aloud. "I think I'd better call Pat Kelly and Father John."

# CHAPTER XLII

"Hello, Pat. Have you a moment to talk?"

"I do, Father. Thanks for calling."

"I assume you've been in touch with the sheriff."

"Last night, yes, but not since. Have you talked to him today?"

"Nothing new – not as of just before my morning Mass. I was wondering how you're doing."

"Strangely, not so well. I mean, I didn't think I'd come to care that much about Wetzel."

"Will it help to talk?"

"It might, yes."

"Do you have time now?"

"I could … in fifteen minutes."

"I'll come over. I have errands to run afterward. See you at your office."

"Fine."

He decided to walk. He'd have time to think about the present state of affairs. Hank was going to be okay, the sheriff had said, and he'd be back tonight. Gil Wetzel had taken three bullets, and his prognosis wasn't good. All the drug people were in custody. But Pat Kelly's feeling troubled about his client was a new and surprising development. He hadn't seen that coming.

Pat's face looked troubled, as his pastor entered the law office across from the courthouse. "You don't look good, Pat," he said, with genuine concern.

"I don't know why, but this shooting has really gotten to me."

"You didn't have much use for him, the sheriff told me."

"I didn't. But it was his sudden turn-around, I guess. I don't know – maybe Goodman's personality is also a part of it. I think I took it to heart that Goodman was, in effect, not treating him any better than Drexel was. Whatever, I really feel for him right now. It troubles me that he's hovering in medical limbo in some hospital."

He looked at Father John's face before speaking again. "I know: he seemed kind of creepy when I first got put with him … and he certainly did some awful things. There's a lot to justify my first reaction. But that change! You'd call it grace, I'm betting, Father."

"You'd be right, Pat. It's grace, all right! And grace is often surprising, even shocking. Its suddenness, what it does to a person, the disguises it sometimes uses, and especially the fact that most of us tend to disregard it in our day-to-day living: all that can make us sitting ducks for being bowled over whenever it shows up somewhere in a person's life. No doubt in my mind: it's grace that erupted in Gil's life a few days ago."

"Well, it's hooked me. I wish there were something I could do for him. But at this distance, I can't even visit him in his room."

"If they'd even let you, Pat! His condition is so iffy, I doubt they'd even be happy about my spending any time with him. I did learn that the hospital chaplain has anointed him. But I don't even know if he's conscious. I was hoping the sheriff would have called today. I have a ton of questions for him."

"Well, I did learn that the feds now don't think they got anything like a 'kingpin' with Drexel. Did you know they were calling him that?"

"No."

"Well, they were, Father. Now what they're saying is that even though this operation was going on for years, it was pretty much penny-ante. I don't know if Drexel was smart enough to keep the drug amounts small, or if he just wasn't greedy, or what … but from what the sheriff was able to get out of Goodman, this wasn't a big drug operation at all. The feds have stopped some trafficking, all right, but their grandiose dreams about removing huge amounts of drugs from our streets don't seem to be accurate."

"But wasn't Gil shot by a 'bodyguard?' Sounds like some sophistication to me."

"I think bodyguard's too highfalutin a term. Drexel had an ordinary home in an ordinary neighborhood, and he ran a modest-sized trucking company. The shooter seems to have been an employee of the trucking company. A bunch of guys in that company were in a local shooting club, and this guy was apparently recruited just for that day as a backup form of protection … in case Wetzel tried something when they nabbed him. They're looking into all those employees now because they figure this one shooter was unafraid to go after people, as opposed to paper targets, and could well have been willing to help 'off' Gilbert. Maybe those other gun club guys were questionable in their morality too. They're checking, I was told last night.

"I didn't get anywhere near the whole story last night, but what the sheriff told me came from Hank, I think, namely, that there wasn't nearly the operation they were expecting … or hoping for, either. No huge number of thugs or drugs, nothing big-fish about it at all.

"Goes without saying that Goodman didn't get much out of this to brag about. And now Gil's somewhere between life and death over some two-bit bunch of criminals! Seems to me that Goodman will have to answer to higher-ups about all the time and money he put into this bring-down. Serves him right! But not Gil!"

"One thing you can do, Pat, is pray for him."

"I have been – ever since the sheriff's call yesterday."

"Good for you! But another thing you could do … "

"What?"

" … is call sheriff Toler right now. Maybe he'll have some news that can bring you out of your funk."

"Good idea." He picked up his phone.

Once on the line with the sheriff, he listened intently for several minutes. Father John was reading his face, and the longer the conversation went on, the worse it looked.

"I'm with Father John right now, Sheriff. I'll tell him and save you a call. Thanks." He turned to the priest. "It's not good."

"I didn't think it was, judging from your face just now. What did he tell you?"

"Wetzel's gotten worse. He's now in intensive care. The arm wound's not much, but the two torso wounds are the problem. There's internal organ damage – spleen, I think he said – and he's running a high temperature. The next twenty-four hours or so are crucial."

"That's awful, all right. I'll call our prayer chain with a special intention. Did the sheriff say anything about the arrests or anything?"

"Goodman told him today that Drexel's rolling over like a trained puppy. They might not have a blockbuster case, but they apparently won't have any trouble getting it handled quickly and completely. And the so-and-so had the insensitivity to suggest to sheriff Toler that they might even luck out further by not having to worry about Wetzel's deal. I hope I never have to mess with him again."

"You mean, he implied that if Wetzel dies, he'd count that as a plus for the feds?"

"That's the way I read it."

"Well, I guess I have to amend my earlier statement. One other surprising thing about grace is where it does *not* strike sometimes."

The men sat glumly, the priest wishing he could help the lawyer but realizing that they were both in the same emotional boat. "Let's pray for a few moments, Pat." The two joined hands and prayed silently before ending with the Our Father.

Father John rose to leave. "Whoever hears something gets back to the other, okay?"

"Right."

"I'll be on some errands awhile but should be back in an hour."

"Okay, Father. Thanks for coming over here."

Father John picked up mail, retrieved the trousers that Googie had fixed from the cleaners and stopped at the Becker Pharmacy. But there were a number of customers inside, and he quickly excused himself to Frieda. Waving to Fred, who had glanced up from his prescriptions, he stepped outside. He was back at St. Helena's well before his self-imposed deadline of an hour.

He had busied himself at his desk for the next two hours and was lost in concentration on his mail when the phone startled him.

"St. Helena's," he said cheerfully.

It was Pat Kelly. "Gil died twenty minutes ago."

# CHAPTER XLIII

Later in June, after he – and Algoma, as well – had largely settled down from the events of the late spring, Father John decided that it was time to bring closure to a few loose ends still dangling since the upheaval those stressful weeks had brought to so many. He called Jim and asked him to gather his friends the next Saturday for a short prayer service at Pete's grave in St. Helena's cemetery. Late morning was agreed on. Next he called Pete's parents. "Can you and your daughters come to the cemetery at 11 next Saturday to pray for Pete?" They were delighted and touched.

He had just celebrated the first of several Masses for Gilbert Wetzel the morning before. He spoke briefly about the need to pray for the souls of *all* the departed and added a few words about Gilbert, in light of the grace-filled ending to his life. He was surprised to see two of the young men's wives and spoke with them afterward. Their husbands had told them of Gilbert's change of soul, so they made time to attend that Mass.

The same day, while the three caught up on news, Fred and Frieda finally talked him into a small ice cream sundae, since his visit to Doctor Wilson had gone so well. Father John made sure that they knew of Gilbert's graced going-forth from this life, knowing that they would help it gradually get around town.

The Smile was back to routine coverage of small-town goings on, and even Bobbie Sue at the bank had shown some concern for the "sad death of that trucker person." Father John knew her to be aware of his crimes and thought that it spoke well for her to nuance the normally black-and-white views of the local folk. And Horace Denver had stopped his pastor one day the week before to say he had sold another of Annie's paintings adding, as an afterthought, that he had said a prayer for poor young Pete Hamilton. Father John was pleasantly surprised.

Summer was definitely upon them as the small group gathered that Saturday morning at Pete's grave, which bore a small pile of unsettled, mounded dirt. The young men were all present when Pete's parents drove up. Their presence was the pleasant and touching surprise Father John had hoped it would be for the still-grieving family.

A slight but very warm breeze was wafting through the small, heavily treed section where Pete was buried. His grave was in the noontime shadow of a huge elm as the sun approached its zenith, but several of the small congregation were occasionally fanning themselves. Pete's sisters had fresh flowers, and the group watched in reverent silence as they took time to arrange them atop his grave.

After learning that Pete's headstone would be placed there in another week, Father John called the group to a prayerful silence before quietly addressing them. "There have been so many twists and turns for all of us these past weeks. Things from out of some mythological left field were confronting us at every turn and mostly bringing sorrow and unrest into our hearts.

"But over my many years I've come to realize that sorrow and joy are but two sides of the same providential coin. Live as long and I have no doubt you'll come to the same awareness. Let me point out the pertinence of that to these past weeks.

"A gruesome death has restored your boyhood friendships. The terror and violence of those few weeks is helping end the terror and violence of drug use for hundreds, if not thousands, in our state. The sad death of your son, Millie and Joe, has galvanized the force of the law locally and statewide. And all the craziness and confusion we suffered in those weeks has miraculously brought an errant soul to grace and offered help to countless victims of unspeakable acts. And we all have been called deeper into reflection on the importance of love in our lives. All these agonies will be birthing more love in us – if, as Jesus said, 'we have eyes to see.'

"Give thanks with me now for the Lord's grace to us, and pledge again to use it well, as we pray Jesus' prayer. Our Father … "

The group stood quietly, staring at the grave before them as Pete's family fought back tears. Father John spoke again. "Pete's grave can call us back to these realizations whenever we choose. Today, perhaps Shakespeare's poetry from his play 'Cymbelline' can frame that reference for us. The quote may be a tad flowery for us, and border on the grandiose, but I think it nonetheless apt here at Pete's place of rest. 'No exorciser harm thee! Nor no witch charm thee! Ghost unlaid forbear thee! Nothing ill come near thee! Quiet consummation have; and renowned be thy grave.'"

"Amen" several of Pete's friends said quietly, and the group broke to wordlessly straggle back to their cars. Father John was left alone at the grave, praying quietly that peace descend into all the troubled hearts in Algoma and especially asking Gilbert Wetzel in his newly-won situation for help to bring that about.